Praise for The Au Pairs: *Skinny-dipping*

"Even more scandal-packed than the first Au Pairs novel!"

—Teenpeople.com

♥

"Hot beach reading."

—Publishers Weekly

♥

"Trashyfabulous."

—Papermag.com

♥

"Another summer of adventures."

—Teenreads.com

♥

"Glamorous au pairs . . . are once again taking the Hamptons by storm. . . . De la Cruz has a knack for perfectly capturing the dialogue, trials and tribulations of these young hipsters."

—New York Post

♥

"This book will be in high demand."

—School Library Journal

also by melissa de la cruz

the au pairs

the au pairs
skinny-dipping

A NOVEL BY

melissa de la cruz

Simon Pulse
New York   London   Toronto   Sydney

ALLOYENTERTAINMENT
Produced by Alloy Entertainment
151 West 26th Street, New York, NY 10001

SIMON PULSE
An imprint of Simon & Schuster Children's Publishing Division
1230 Avenue of the Americas, New York, NY 10020
Text copyright © 2005 by Alloy Entertainment and Melissa de la Cruz
All rights reserved, including the right of reproduction in whole or
in part in any form.
SIMON PULSE and colophon are registered trademarks
of Simon & Schuster, Inc.
Also available in a Simon & Schuster Books for Young Readers
hardcover edition.
Designed by Christopher Grassi
The text of this book was set in Adobe Garamond.
Manufactured in the United States of America
First Simon Pulse edition June 2006
10 9 8 7 6 5 4 3
The Library of Congress has cataloged the hardcover edition as follows:
De la Cruz, Melissa, 1971–
Skinny-dipping / by Melissa de la Cruz.
p. cm.
"The au pairs."
Summary: When Eliza lands an internship at a club, Mara, Eliza, and Jacqui are annoyed until they learn that the new au pair, Philippe, is gorgeous, French, and male, which is only one of the complications their friendship will have to endure during their summer in the Hamptons.
ISBN-13: 978-1-4169-0382-6 (hc)
ISBN-10: 1-4169-0382-8 (hc)
[1. Au pairs—Fiction. 2. Wealth—Fiction. 3. Friendship—Fiction. 4. Hamptons (N.Y.)—Fiction.] I. Title.
PZ7.D36967Ski 2006
[Fic]—dc22
2005279549
ISBN-13: 978-1-4169-0383-3 (pbk)
ISBN-10: 1-4169-0383-6 (pbk)

This book is lovingly dedicated to Jennie Kim, because you can't write about best friends without having one of your own; Sara Shandler, editor extraordinaire, because this book is as much hers as it is mine; and Mike Johnston, just because.

"It is more shameful to distrust one's friends than to be deceived by them."
—La Rochefoucauld

"It's gettin' hot in herre."

—Nelly

eliza discovers
fire & brimstone is
a new cosmo flavor

IT DIDN'T LOOK LIKE MUCH, BUT THEN THAT WAS PROBABLY because it was three o'clock in the afternoon, and Seventh Circle, the newest, soon-to-be-hottest club in the Hamptons, wouldn't get going until after midnight. A potato barn in its former life, Seventh Circle was a large, brown-shingled, rambling wood building set back in the Southampton woods. Only a discreet sign off the highway (seven circles posted to a tree, natch) let the initiated know they had arrived at their destination.

Eliza Thompson steered her black Jetta into the parking lot, feeling at once pleased and apprehensive. She examined her makeup in the rearview mirror, applied a thick layer of lip gloss, stuck two fingers inside her mouth, and pulled them out slowly, just like *Allure* suggested, in order to avoid a grandmotheresque lipstick-on-teeth situation.

She checked for detritus of Chanel Glossimer. Nothing. Perfect.

Eliza grabbed her bag—the season's covetable metallic leather Balenciaga motorcycle clutch. Eliza had bought it in Palm Beach, during the week she'd spent as a vacation au pair for the Perrys last winter. Inside was a rolled-up resume that listed her sparkling attributes: a Spence education (up until her parents' bankruptcy last year and their subsequent move to Buffalo, that is), an internship at *Jane* (which had entailed fetching nonfat soy lattes and alphabetizing glitter nail polish), and a reference from her longtime friend and Manhattan boy-about-town, Kit Ashleigh.

Life was almost great again for Eliza. Okay, sure, the Thompsons were still living in Buffalo—a far, far cry from the posh life they'd left behind in New York City—but they had moved from a sordid little rental to a proper three-bedroom condominium in the only luxury high-rise in the city. With a little help from some old friends and loyal clients, her dad was slowly getting back on his feet, and there was money for such things as thousand-dollar handbags again. (Well, there was credit at least.) With her grades and SAT scores (top 99th percentile—Eliza was no dummy), there was a good chance she would be able to wing financial aid and get into Princeton after all. This summer her parents were even renting a little Cape Cod in Westhampton. It had the smallest pool Eliza had ever seen—it was practically a bathtub!—but still, it was a house, it was theirs (for the summer), and it was in the Hamptons.

The only thing keeping Eliza off balance was the Big Palm Beach Secret from last winter. Something had happened while she was there that she'd rather forget, but news traveled fast in the Hamptons and Eliza knew she'd have to come clean soon enough.

She brushed aside the thought for now—it was time to focus on the task at hand: getting a job in the hottest new club in the Hamptons and recapturing her title as the coolest girl in town.

Before Buffalo and bankruptcy, Eliza had been famous for being the prettiest, most popular girl on the New York private school circuit. Sugar Perry, who now ruled in her stead, had been a mere wannabe when Eliza was on the scene. Eliza was the one who set the trends (white-blond highlights), knew about all the best parties (Tuesdays at Butter), and dated the hottest guys (polo-playing Charlie Borshok, who was now Sugar's boyfriend as well). Being "outed" as a poor au pair last summer had changed all that, but this was a new year, a new summer, and a new Eliza—who just happened to look a lot like the *old* Eliza, the girl everyone wanted to know and all the other girls wanted to *be*.

It was still drizzling, the end of a typical early June East End rainstorm, as Eliza slid quickly out of her Jetta, which she'd begged her parents to lease her for the summer, and checked her cell phone for any missed calls from Jeremy. Last summer, Eliza had fallen in love with Jeremy Stone, the Perrys' hunky nineteen-year-old gardener, but they'd broken up over the winter since they lived so far away from each other. Now that summer was here, Eliza was dying to see him again. She wasn't exactly sure where Jeremy would fit in with her plans for getting back on top of the social scene, since he wasn't rich or famous (although he was very, very cute), but she did know her plans *included* him, and she hoped that would be good enough. With no missed calls or new texts, Eliza stuffed her phone back in her clutch and headed toward the club.

The door was hanging open, so she let herself inside. Seventh Circle was supposed to be *the* place to be this summer, but here it was, a week after Memorial Day, and it hadn't even opened yet. There was a thick layer of fresh sawdust on the floor, and a full construction crew was barking orders at one another. The barn had been retrofitted to accommodate a U-shaped zinc bar, and against the back wall stood a built-in glass liquor cabinet almost twenty-five feet high. The guys looked up when they spied Eliza. Several whistled at the sight of her tanned legs underneath her pink smocked Juicy tube dress. It was the kind of dress that made everyone else who wore it look fat or pregnant, but on Eliza it looked cute and sexy.

"Hi, I'm here to see the owners—Alan or Kartik?" Eliza said, pulling her long blond hair into a high ponytail.

One of the hard hats grunted and pointed a finger toward the back of the club. Eliza stepped over a paint tray delicately, picking her way past the sawhorses and a couple of dusty potato sacks, toward two guys yammering into their cell phone headsets.

They were the self-styled kings of Manhattan nightlife, and while their press clippings might reach to the ceiling, neither was taller than five-five, and Eliza towered over both of them in her four-inch Louboutin platforms. Alan Whitman was balding and dough-faced, but he'd been legendary since ninth grade at Riverdale, when he'd begun his career selling pot at the Limelight.

He'd oozed his way up a string of downtown hot spots until he'd raised enough money to open his trio of celebrity playgrounds—Vice, Circus, and Lowdown. He liked to say that before he'd gotten his hands on Paris Hilton, she was just a cute little Dwight sophomore in a rolled-up uniform skirt. He'd been the one who'd waived Paris past the ID check and had personally alerted gossip columnists when she was dancing on the tables—or falling off them—on any given night. His partner, Kartik (one name only), a Miami transplant, had been friends with Madonna back when he was still a teenager and she was still a dog-collar-wearing pop icon, not a dowdy children's book author who answered to the name Esther.

"What do you mean the liquor license is delayed? Are you serious?" Alan whined into his receiver.

"Babycakes, of course we've got the permits in hand," Kartik smoothly promised on his cell. "We're ready to roll. We're all set for the after-party, no problem!"

Eliza stood aside patiently, watching the guys tell two different stories on their phones. It was inspirational, really: If Alan Whitman could transform himself from some geeky kid who sold oregano dime bags out of his Eastman backpack into New York's most sought-after nightclub promoter, then surely she, Eliza Thompson, could find a way to reinvent herself from fallen Manhattan It Girl into Hamptons royalty. After all, Eliza had always wanted to be a princess.

mara goes from zero to somebody in sixty seconds

THE STRETCH LIMOUSINE IN HER DRIVEWAY WAS THE FIRST sign that for Mara Waters, life was going to start getting interesting again. During prom season in Sturbridge, it wasn't unusual to find rented limos parked in front of the tidy ranch-style houses, but this one didn't sport a CALL 1-800 DISCO LIMO! sticker on its bumper. Instead, it had a uniformed chauffeur who held a golf umbrella above Mara's head and took her bags from her stupefied father.

Anna Perry had told Mara she would send a car, but Mara hadn't been expecting one quite so large and luxurious. Then again, everything that Anna Perry, the very young, very demanding second wife of Kevin Perry, one of New York's most successful and feared litigators in New York City, did was patently over-the-top. Anna had wanted Mara in East Hampton immediately, and whatever Anna wanted, Anna usually got. She'd convinced their new neighbors, the Reynolds family, who were leaving Cape Cod for the Hamptons in their private plane, to give Mara a ride.

Heading back to the Hamptons on a private jet was the complete opposite of last August, when Mara had returned to Sturbridge on a battered Greyhound. It had been the summer of her life, and she'd made the best friends in the world—Eliza, an uptight Upper East Side golden girl, and Jacqui, a Brazilian bombshell so beautiful men routinely threw themselves at her feet. They'd all signed on for a summer of babysitting the Perry kids—to the tune of ten thousand dollars for the summer—but the friendship they formed was even more valuable. The three of them were as different as could be, but somewhere between the social climbing, the party crashing, and keeping all the kids in line, the three of them had formed a tight-knit bond.

There was another reason that last summer had been amazing: Ryan Perry. She'd fallen completely in love with Ryan, the older brother of the kids she was babysitting, and they'd finally gotten together the last week of the summer. When they said good-bye, Mara had told him that she would love to bring him home so he could meet her family and see where she lived. But when she got off the Greyhound at the grimy Sturbridge bus stop several hours later, it no longer seemed like a good idea.

Her stomach had sunk when Megan picked her up in their dented '88 Ford Taurus. Mara was still wearing her Hamptons uniform: a lace-trimmed silk camisole, pre-faded cargo pants and high-heeled jewel-encrusted mules from Miss Trish of Capri. Her hair still smelled of Eliza's French lavender shampoo, but the sight of the car and her sister brought reality home to her. Mara had never been ashamed or embarrassed of where she came from, but after a summer in the Hamptons, she suddenly thought, *This isn't good enough*. He came from a family that hired a personal chef, and she came from a family with a fifteen-year-old microwave.

She'd made a bunch of excuses to put off Ryan's visit to Sturbridge, telling him she had to study for a test or had to write a paper. Finally, in November, she'd taken the train to Groton to visit him at his fancy private school. But she'd been awkward and out of place among his friends, and she'd broken up with him the next week, telling him what she'd been telling herself ever since she got back to Sturbridge: Last summer was fun and all, but it wasn't real life. They weren't meant to be.

But breaking up with Ryan Perry and forgetting about Ryan Perry were two different things altogether. She couldn't stop thinking about him, and a secret part of her wished that he'd tried harder to change her mind. He'd been totally understanding about their breakup, but that was the problem: Ryan was almost too nice. If only he'd yelled, or cried, or fought for their relation-ship more. Maybe that was all she'd wanted—to hear that he really missed her, really needed her. But he hadn't said anything, only, "If this is what you really want," and she'd told him it was. So it was over, and she hadn't heard from Ryan since.

She'd excused herself from babysitting for the Perrys in Palm Beach over winter break, fearing it would be too weird to see Ryan. But as winter turned to spring, Mara still couldn't get Ryan out of her head, and she realized what a mistake breaking up with him had been. She was still in love with him, and when Anna Perry had called to offer Mara her old job (along with a raise—twelve thousand dollars for the summer!), Mara had started planning the outfit she'd wear when she first saw Ryan and how they'd fall into each other's arms and pretend the year apart had never happened. She'd played the scene in her head so many times, she'd really started to believe it would happen.

It rained all the way on the drive to Barnstable, a private airfield in Hyannis, and the car drove right up to the tarmac, where a white tent and a red carpet led to a sleek silver plane emblazoned with a gleaming *R* logo on the wing. A flight attendant in a crisp navy blue uniform took Mara's bags—last year's treasured LL Bean totes—and Mara was momentarily flustered to realize that the rest of the luggage cart held sleek nylon-and-canvas rollaway suitcases. Would she ever get it right?

A tall lady in an embroidered caftan and raffia slippers wearing the biggest diamond Mara had ever seen cheerfully waved her up the ramp. "Pity about the rain, isn't it? They said it would shower—but this is almost a hurricane! I'm Chelsea Reynolds, welcome, welcome. There you go, watch the puddle on the last step. Anna told me we were picking up a friend, but she didn't say it was *you*!"

Her? Mara didn't know what she meant by that, and was about to ask, but the minute she set foot inside the plane, she was enveloped in a bear hug.

"If it isn't Miss Waters! The diva! Girlfriend, where've you been all year?" Lucky Yap demanded, readjusting his own leopard-print dashiki. Lucky was one of the most important paparazzi working the society circuit. He was the unofficial arbiter of Hamptons fabulosity—if you were in, Lucky took your photo; if you were out, you might as well move to the Jersey shore.

"Lucky, hi!" Mara smiled, surrendering to his flurry of air-kisses.

Lucky handed her a glass of champagne and quickly introduced her to the rest of the passengers—a typical hoity-toity Hamptons crowd wearing similar variations on ethnic African tribal wear. Apparently, the Serengeti had relocated to the East End this year. There was a smattering of boldfaced names and their assorted hangers-on, from brand-name heiresses to well-preserved society swans to pretty public-relations assistants and the E! style experts they represented.

"Everyone knows Mara, right? My muse?" Lucky brayed. Last summer, Mara had helped Lucky out on a tricky assignment, and the popular photographer had made her a perennial presence in the society pages to show his appreciation.

"Of course!" a sweet-faced girl replied. "Didn't we meet at the Polo last year?"

"Love that shirt. Is it Proenza?" one of the style experts asked, fingering the material on her pink polka-dot blouse. She'd matched it with a pair of slim white Bermuda shorts and cork-wedge espadrilles. After spending last summer with two fashion mavens—Jacqui and Eliza—Mara had picked up a few tips. She was flattered by the compliment and didn't have the heart to tell him it was a knockoff she'd bought at Forever 21 for fifteen bucks.

Lucky took a few shots of her, then leaned over to whisper conspiratorially with his seatmate. Mara couldn't help but over-hear buzzing as her name was linked to Ryan Perry's.

The stewardess led her to the nearest available seat and Mara sipped happily from her champagne flute, soaking in the atmos-phere, listening in on the gossip from the Cape Cod beach wed-ding they were all returning from. After a year in Sturbridge, where the most glamorous thing in town was the hokey piano bar attached to the Hyatt, she'd forgotten how well the other half lived.

"Oh! There's Garrett!" a girl next to Mara whispered excitedly.

"Mr. Reynolds!" Lucky greeted. "Can we get a shot?"

Mara looked up to see a tall, shaggy-haired boy emerge from the cockpit. Immediately, all the girls in the group stood up a little straighter, trying to catch his eye. He was holding a cham-pagne bottle aloft and grinning. He was rakishly, devilishly hand-some, with a Jude Law-style flop of dark hair falling over his forehead. His button-down white Thomas Pink shirt lay rumpled and untucked from his black wool pants.

"You," he said, walking down the aisle and heading straight for Mara.

He had deep, dark eyes, as dark as his hair, framed by the thickest set of lashes Mara had ever seen. "Come with me," he said, taking her by the hand before she could protest. As Garrett led her away, the group parted silently to let them through, and Mara received glances of barely contained jealousy from the girls, as well as an approving nod from Lucky. Mara felt singled out, special, and she couldn't help but think, *Hamptons, here I come.*

jacqui gets serious . . .
about shopping

THE GUY AT BOOKHAMPTON WAVED AWAY HER CHARGE
card with a smile, even though Jacqui Velasco insisted on paying
for her books herself. Just once she wished she could meet a guy
who saw past her *Sports Illustrated* Swimsuit Edition body. It was
getting on her nerves a little—the abject, puppy-dog treatment
from men who were always more than willing to pick up the
check, the tab, the bill. Not too long ago, Jacqui was more than
happy to let them pay, and she had a wardrobe full of Louis
Vuitton, Gucci, and Prada to prove it. But things were different
now. Last summer, Jacqui's heart had been broken by slimy Luke
van Varick, and now she was determined to become a more serious person, someone whom people took seriously.

"*Por favor,* I insist," Jacqui repeated, trying to change his mind.

"Sorry, your money's no good here," the pimply cashier
repeated, even though Jacqui knew he'd hear it from his boss later
when the receipts came up short. But that was the impact Jacqui
had on guys—something about her slightly almond-shaped eyes

and bee-stung lips (not to mention that impressive set of 36Cs) turned even a ninety-pound bookstore nerd into a protective, macho, chest-puffing buffoon who would do anything to impress her. "Consider it a gift," he added.

Jacqui sighed and accepted the plastic bag reluctantly, tossing it into her patent leather carryall. She walked into the bright early-summer afternoon and crossed the street to sit on a park bench to wait for Eliza. It was another glorious day in East Hampton. The early-morning rainfall had given way to sparkling sunshine, and the tiny, jewel-box boutiques on Main Street trilled with the chatter of what to wear to another season of beachfront barbecues and white-tent benefits. Jacqui was oblivious to the stares from the preening slicksters in their 911 Carreras or the head-to-toe scrutiny from the Botox brigade. She sat and immediately immersed herself in her book, *The U.S. News & World Report*'s guide to America's best colleges.

It was amazing what a little studying could do for her grades and how gratifying it was to bring home a decent report card for a change. Her grandmother couldn't believe it—during the past year, Jacqui had spent more time at the library than the mall and was even talking about going to college. In the past, the only thing Jacqui had been passionate about was whether or not she'd be able to score the latest fox-fur Prada shrug before anyone else. Before, she'd had only a vague idea of what she wanted for the future. She'd always assumed she'd end up marrying some rich guy twice her age and spend the rest of her life flitting between spa treatments and couture fittings while ignoring her husband's infidelities. It was the life that Jacqui had been groomed for.

Her mother, a former beauty queen who had won third runner-up in a Miss Universe pageant, once had her pick of suitors—from the son of the owner of the largest electric company in the country, to the son of a landed cattle rancher. Instead, she'd settled on a handsome civil engineer with beautiful black eyes and no family money whatsoever. Roberto Velasco was resolutely middle-class in a country of extreme wealth and extreme poverty. The Velascos lived happily enough in Campinas, and her mother contented herself with ruling over the small provincial society, but she wanted more for her daughter, which was why she'd sent Jacqui to live with her grandmother in São Paulo to attend a private school in the city where Jacqui would rub shoulders with the daughters of the ruling *branco* class.

But Jacqui's beautiful face and Coke-bottle curves had only made the rich girls envious, and Jacqui had made few friends there. For a while, she'd dutifully dated the arrogant scions of landowners and the sugarcane gentry, but that soon bored her, and she'd found that true adventure lay in the arms of their married, older fathers.

Then Luke van Varick—her Luca—had come into her life. A cool American boy with a lazy grin and a huge backpack, she'd met him while he was traveling over spring break and had fallen hard for him. After their two-week spring fling, he'd told her he loved her and then disappeared. She'd tracked him down all the way to the Hamptons, but it turned out her Luca had actually belonged to someone else the whole time.

So now Jacqui had a better plan: She would do a great job for the Perrys this summer so they would recommend her as a live-in nanny for one of their rich friends. That way she could move to New York City for her senior year of high school and go to Stuyvesant, an elite public school in the city, through their foreign-exchange program. If she did well there, she'd have a chance to attend NYU and make something of her life. She had Eliza's friend Kit to thank for putting the idea in her head when they'd hung out together in Palm Beach over winter break. He'd told her about his older sister, who hadn't done a lick of work at school until senior year and was now a freshman at NYU.

In order to make her dreams happen, Jacqui had made a bunch of new rules for herself, the most important being No More Boys. They were just distractions, and if Jacqui had been able to resist the temptations of the cutest guys in Brazil, she could definitely do the same in the Hamptons. She was going to keep her head down, take care of those kids, and attend an SAT prep class on her nights off. God help her, she was going to show the world she was more than just an empty-headed Gisele clone.

She perused the pages of the guidebook: There were photographs of sweater-wearing coeds sitting on green lawns, and an endless array of statistics concerning minority enrollment, merit scholarships, and alumni testimonials. Okay, so it was just a teensy bit boring. Surely there was something else she could do while waiting. She slammed the book shut and looked at her watch. Eliza was due to pick her up in a half hour, and Scoop looked awfully inviting across the street. Just because she was getting serious about school didn't mean she couldn't indulge in her favorite extracurricular activity, did it?

A girl's got to have a new bikini, after all.

eliza learns that hell is made for famous people

"YOU GOT ANY EXPERIENCE WITH NIGHTCLUBS?" ALAN Whitman asked, once the three of them were seated on plastic-wrapped leather club chairs in the back of the room. He had barely glanced at the resume Eliza had handed him. To Eliza's chagrin, her chair made a squishy, sticky sound like an embarrassing bodily function whenever she moved. Thankfully, neither of the guys seemed to notice.

"Not specifically," she replied. "But I'm really eager to learn. I read in the *Times* that you guys are looking to expand into publicity, marketing, and upscale lifestyle branding, and that's really where I see myself making a—"

"Do you know any celebrities? High-profile people?" Kartik interrupted with an intense look on his face as he put the tops of his fingers together in an upside-down V-shape without his palms touching.

"Uh . . ." Eliza said warily.

"Like Jessica and Ashlee? Or the Perry twins?"

"Of course, we went—I mean, we go to school together," she said, relieved.

"Who doesn't? But that's good. Because we really need that kind of crowd here," Kartik said, frowning. "There are five new nightclubs opening this summer, and we need to have the hottest people here. I don't want to see has-beens, nobodies, fuglies. I want to see Mary-Kate Olsen puking in the bathroom, if you know what I mean."

Eliza nodded.

Alan hooted. "Damn, Kartik, don't be so hard on her just because she blew you off!"

His partner ignored him, boring his eyes into Eliza. "I can't tell you how important it is to get someone in here who recognizes everyone from Tara Reid to Page Six reporters. You've got to know the scene." He paused meaningfully. "We had a kid at Vice who didn't let JC Chasez in! I mean, I know it's hard to recognize those 'N Sync guys without Justin, but man, did I hear about it then. You know, when it's kicking, this place is going to be like Beverly Hills, SoHo, and Saint-Tropez combined, but on the beach to boot!"

Eliza didn't bother to point out that Saint-Tropez *was* on the beach.

"It's a real demanding position. You're like the quarterback driving up the lane," Alan interjected, mangling his sports metaphors. "Every night in Seventh Circle is going to be the center of the freaking universe, you know what I mean? That's the way we operate. Like a freaking constellation of stars!" He slammed his fist on the zinc-topped coffee table.

"Here's the deal," Kartik said pompously. "This place is all about celebs. Without celebs, we don't get the mooks who pay the thirty-dollar entrance fee to gawk at 'em."

Alan nodded wisely, adding, "Overpriced, watered-down, six-ounce cocktails taste that much sweeter if Chauncey Raven's at the next table fondling her new husband. So, invite the Perry twins, give them a table, make sure it's one up on the second level where they can see everybody and everybody can see them. Keep. The. Celebrities. Happy. Dig?"

"Anything they want, anything!" Kartik said, picking up the refrain, and it dawned on Eliza that she was watching a carefully choreographed song-and-dance routine. "Lindsey Lohan wants a pizza from Domino's at 3 A.M.? *Done!* Avril Lavigne needs a private helicopter back to the city? *Done!* R. Kelly wants a stripper for his birthday party? *Double-done!*" He punched the air to emphasize his point.

Eliza nodded briskly. At the magazine, during a celebrity shoot, she'd once had to fill a toilet bowl with gardenias every time the diva went to the bathroom, so she was used to catering to a set of ridiculous demands.

"Of course, the rules change for civilians," Alan said in a silky tone. "If it's a group of guys, double the drink bill—they'll never notice. Keep the tables turning, unless they've reserved it for the entire summer, and in that case, keep the five-hundred-dollar bottles moving, at least two per hour, 'cause that's what's going to pay the overhead."

"Remember, you've got to dress sexy, look sexy, feel sexy, you know?" Kartik grinned. "Here's a piece of advice: The shorter the skirt, the better the tips. I'm talking crotch-length, babe," he said, making a cutting motion with his hand across his thigh to demonstrate.

Alan reached out to grab her elbow, making Eliza recoil. "Whatever you do, never, never, never, ever, ever, *ever* let anybody in if they're not on the list. The list is God. It could be my mother out there, but if she's not on the list, tough luck, Ma, no list, no entry. Unless it's a celeb, but that goes without saying. I'm frigging serious. The only way we can keep the place hot is if absolutely no one can get in."

A model in a baby T-shirt and ripped jeans slunk out of the bathroom and plopped herself on the armrest of Alan's chair. "Baby, I'm hungry," she pouted. Eliza recognized her from a recent Victoria's Secret commercial. She'd been wearing a lace teddy and three-foot-long angel wings. The ad always irritated Eliza—what kind of lame sexual fantasy involved underwear and hokey feather-covered appendages?

"Get the chef to make you something," Alan said irritably.

"I love your necklace," the model said in a thick accent, flicking her eyes at Eliza.

Eliza nodded. "Thanks." She fiddled with the leather string Ryan had given her in Palm Beach, feeling a pang of anxiety.

"What do you think? You up for it?" Kartik asked. "The best summer of your life?"

Eliza smiled, thinking she'd heard that line before. "When do I start?" she asked, elated that she'd landed the job so easily. She would be back on the A-list as fast as you could say, "By invitation only."

"Saturday," Alan and Kartik replied in unison.

"In two days?" Eliza blanched, looking around. Hello, the walls were still exposed Sheetrock, weren't they?

"Relax. It's only a soft opening, for a premiere party. You know that new movie that's an update of *Gone with the Wind* with Jennifer Love Hewitt and Chad Michael Murray? Favor for a friend of ours. You know Mitzi Goober?" Kartik asked.

Eliza nodded. Mitzi was only the most feared publicist in the tristate area. At twenty-seven Mitzi had achieved immortality by landing on the cover of *New York* magazine as a "party grrrrl." Two years ago she'd spent a month in jail after her teacup Chihuahua attacked an unsuspecting waitress's fur-trimmed uniform vest, landing the waitress in the hospital and Mitzi on the cover of the tabloids. It was widely reported that Mitzi had laughed off the incident and called the waitress a "fashion victim," setting off a class war that resulted in aggressive and diminutive canines being banned from certain Hamptons eateries. But now she was back, a bestselling prison memoir under her belt, and more popular than ever. It was the Paris Hilton effect—there was no such thing as bad publicity in the Hamptons.

"But . . ." Eliza wordlessly motioned to the surrounding mess. It was hard to believe that in less than forty-eight hours the place would be turned into something resembling a decent watering hole.

"They'll be done by then, I promise you. By the way, how old are you?"

"I just turned seventeen . . ." she said tentatively, wondering if she should have lied.

Kartik waved a hand dismissively. "You're not bartending, so it's cool."

Eliza realized she didn't know what exactly she would be doing, or even how much she would be making. It seemed a little rude to ask, especially since the interview was obviously over. She figured they would straighten out those details later.

"You guys fans of Dante?" she asked, on her way out the door.

"Huh?" Kartik looked at her blankly. Alan was already nuzzling the underage panty model, his hands disappearing up the back of her shirt.

"The club. Seventh Circle. It's about the seventh circle of hell, right?" she asked, wondering if she sounded like an idiot, because that was how her new boss was looking at her. She remembered from English class that in Dante's *Inferno*, the seventh circle of hell was where Alexander the Great, Attila the Hun, and a bunch of other boldface names in history had ended up, due to sins of violence and pride.

"Sure, whatever." He shrugged. "Dante's cool. He's that new DJ from Paris, right?"

Eliza made a note that being literate was something that her new job—whatever it was—would not entail. Just wear the short skirt and keep the celebrities happy. She could do that.

is there such a thing as an accidental lap dance?

"I'M MARA, BY THE WAY," MARA SAID TO THE DARK-HAIRED boy who was uncorking a champagne bottle. She wondered why he was paying so much attention to her—there were several girls on board who made their living off their cheekbones, and yet he'd barely looked at them. The two of them were sitting opposite each other in cushy caramel leather wing chairs in a cozy alcove behind the cockpit.

"I know who you are," he said smoothly. "You work for the Perrys, right? I'm Garrett Reynolds," he introduced himself, offering a hand. Mara had already put two and two together. It was his parents' jet. They were *that* Reynolds family. The one *Forbes* magazine had just minted America's newest billionaires. His father, Ezra Reynolds, was responsible for littering the Manhattan skyline with *R* logos on all of his buildings.

Garrett pulled down a cantilevered metal table hidden in a side panel and began placing champagne glasses in two rows on top of it, taking the glasses out of an adjoining cabinet. The flight attendants secured the doors and the plane began to roll down the runway. Mara noticed there was no standard spiel concerning safety procedures, the nearest exits, or about using one's seat cushion as a floatation device (although she bet mink didn't float). She and Garrett were two of the few people even sitting down.

"It looks pretty bad out there," Mara noted, as the storm rattled the plane.

"We're only a half-point over the minimums to fly," Garrett agreed, explaining that unlike commercial airlines, which were legally required to adhere to FAA regulations that restricted flying under certain weather conditions—like, say, the violent downpour they were caught in—private jets had no such limitations. As long as wind velocity met a minimum standard, they were good to go. "But apparently Mother has a hair appointment she can't miss." Garrett smirked.

Mara didn't know if he was kidding or not. That Chelsea Reynolds would risk death for a blowout was totally plausible, considering everything Mara knew about the Hamptons high life.

"Brace yourself," Garrett warned, cupping the magnum of champagne under his chin.

The plane took off like a bumper car on a trampoline, and Mara heard the crowd shriek with laughter as they bounced around like pinballs. Miraculously, none of the glassware on their table moved an inch.

"Magnetized bottoms." Garrett smiled, pouring champagne into each flute as the plane zigzagged off the ground.

Mara gripped her armrest worriedly, but Garrett seemed completely oblivious to the booming thunder and taut drumbeat of the raindrops against the windowpanes.

"Is it always this, uh, bouncy?" Mara asked, trying desperately to keep her balance on her seat as the plane hit a sharp air pocket. If there was a seat belt, she couldn't find it.

"Smaller planes take the bumps harder on takeoff, although this weather certainly doesn't help," he mused. "This is nothing compared to landing," he added.

When all the champagne flutes were filled to the brim with bubbly, Garrett looked up at her expectantly. Mara couldn't help but be reminded of the way her cat Stinky always stared at Blue, her sister's parakeet.

"There's an old saying in the West . . ." Garrett drawled, leaning forward and staring into her eyes intently.

Mara smirked. So that explained why he'd chosen her. It was all a game called Let's Get the New Girl Drunk. Did he really think she would be such an easy mark? In Sturbridge, they'd used beer mugs instead of champagne flutes, but she was sure the rules were the same.

"In Texas, it's always high noon," Mara replied somberly, gratified when Garrett nodded admiringly at her recognition of the game's ritual introduction.

"And at high noon, we . . . *draw*!" Garrett exclaimed, reaching for his first flute.

Mara lunged for hers. She opened her throat and poured the sharp, crisp liquid inside.

"Draw again!" Garrett exclaimed gleefully when he'd emptied his glass before she was even halfway through hers.

Mara slammed her flute down, surprised she'd been beaten, and promptly reached for another. She won the next round, barely, but Garrett beat her on every other, until each glass on her side was empty. Damn, this guy was slick. In Sturbridge, Mara had wiped the floor with many a competitor, putting even the most funnel-happy football player to shame. Her ex-boyfriend Jim had taught her that the trick was not to breathe.

"Impressive," she commended him.

"Thank you," Garrett smiled. "You're not so bad yourself."

Mara relaxed against her seat, momentarily forgetting her nervousness about the turbulence, when a particularly sharp jolt threw her completely out of her chair and onto his lap.

"Oh my God! I'm so sorry!" she exclaimed, scrambling to get her balance.

"No need to apologize," Garrett replied breezily, helping Mara steady herself against him when the plane bounced sharply again. She clung to him, bouncing up and down against his lap.

"So you're that kind of girl," Garrett joked, making her blush. He was obnoxious, but somehow charming all the same. She couldn't help but notice how tightly he was holding her.

"You're driving me crazy," he growled, half-mockingly, but with a flirtatious edge. "Why don't you have dinner with me this weekend? That way, we can actually get to know each other instead of just fooling around like this."

"I can't." She shook her head. "I have to work, I'm sorry." She wondered what Ryan would think if he saw her now, sitting on some other boy's lap.

"I'm making the reservation anyway." He shrugged. "I'll pretend I didn't hear that."

A few minutes later, the plane stopped shaking and the pilot announced that they were above the storm clouds and had settled into a stable cruising altitude. Garrett helped Mara to her seat, bowing and kissing her hand in a gentlemanly fashion. She exhaled a sigh of relief when he excused himself to attend to his other guests. He was suave all right, but she had a feeling Garrett Reynolds always got—or bought—what he wanted, and Mara was definitely not for sale.

in girl-talk,
"you look great!"
means "i'm so happy
to see you"

INSIDE SCOOP, JACQUI TREATED THE DRESSING ROOM as a revolving door, posing in each skimpy bathing suit in rapid succession, discarding those that were too tight across the chest and too small in back. (She'd gotten in trouble for her thongs on Georgica Beach last year, and she didn't want to get hauled in again for violating the "morality" laws that kept the Hamptons beaches safe from the sight of exposed rear ends.) When Eliza found her, she was wearing a bandeau top and checking out the crucial crack-covering ability of a minuscule suit bottom by performing a series of squats in front of the three-way mirror (to the obvious consternation of an envious row of shoppers).

"Sorry, am I interrupting?" Eliza joked, as Jacqui performed deep knee bends in the tiny half-moon piece of fabric.

"'Liza!" Jacqui said happily, standing up for a hug. They embraced each other warmly, Eliza's stack of gold bangle bracelets clanking against Jacqui's bare shoulders.

"Look at you!" Eliza said, pulling Jacqui's arms out and admiring how her friend filled out the Gaultier bikini.

"No, *chica*, look at you!" Jacqui squealed. The two of them clucked and cooed in the fawning, joyful way that girls greet each other, effusively complimenting each other on their hair, their shoes, their weight loss (real or imagined).

"I didn't see you at the Jitney stop and figured you'd be here," Eliza explained. "I'm sorry I'm late. The interview took a while."

"How did it go?" Jacqui asked, disappearing into the dressing room to change.

"Awesome! I got the job!" Eliza said, admiring a canvas Kate Spade tote.

"Hooray!" Jacqui cheered, emerging in a bohemian-style empire-waist dress and high-heeled Gucci clogs. "Do you take AmEx?" she asked the salesgirl, handing her the bikini.

"Can I take a quick peek around before we get Mara?" Eliza asked, critically examining a crocheted poncho while Jacqui paid for her new purchase.

"I think her plane gets in right now, so no."

"All riiiiight," Eliza said, looking longingly at the brightly colored Matthew Williamson sarongs. "We'll come back."

"So, how've you been?" Jacqui asked, when they were in Eliza's car on the way to the East Hampton airport. They rolled down all the windows to let in the fresh ocean breeze, even though Eliza had the AC cranking. The girls hadn't seen each other since Palm Beach, where they'd shopped on Worth Avenue and hung out at the Four Seasons pool with all the kids in tow. There'd been an insane Christmas ball at the Colony Club and a lavish New Year's party at the Breakers. Everything had been perfect—except for the fact that Mara hadn't joined them. Jacqui couldn't wait for all three of them to be back together again soon, but first she wanted to make sure Eliza had come clean about what exactly had happened when Mara *wasn't* around.

"I'm good." Eliza nodded, and told Jacqui about her plans for world (or at least Hamptons) domination that summer. She was going to be working at the coolest club and hanging out with the hottest people—in her mind, it wasn't even a job, it was more like . . . a title, a position. She would be *representing* what Seventh Circle was all about. Her old crew would come around, and soon she'd be calling the shots again. She had nothing to be embarrassed about this summer, and she was counting on her connection with Kartik and Alan to facilitate her return to the high life.

"Have you seen Ryan yet?" Jacqui asked, steering the conversation back to where she wanted it to go.

"No, but we've e-mailed, and I spoke to him on the phone the other night. I don't think it'll be awkward." Eliza had tried to push the memory out of her mind, but the fact that she'd hooked up with Ryan Perry—the love of her best friend's life—in Palm Beach was not easily forgotten. Especially when she had yet to tell that best friend. "I mean, it was just a stupid drunken thing, and we've been friends for, like, ever."

After Sugar and Poppy Perry's New Year's party at the

Breakers, Eliza and Ryan had gone back to the hotel so that Eliza could pick up some flip-flops, since her Louboutins were killing her. They were both completely smashed from the champagne, and for the first time on vacation they were both happy. Ryan had been sad because Mara had broken up with him and backed out of Palm Beach, and Eliza was depressed because Jeremy had told her they should take a break until next summer, since being away from each other was so hard. Ryan found *The Godfather* on pay-per-view and they snuggled next to each other on the bed, just like when they were kids and had memorized all the lines.

"Leave the gun, take the cannoli," they said at the same time, and they both laughed. Then, all of a sudden, he was kissing her . . . or she was kissing him . . . and then they were totally fooling around. They hadn't meant it to happen, and it didn't mean *anything*, she swore.

"I'm going to tell Mara as soon as I see her," Eliza said emphatically, clenching the steering wheel so hard her knuckles turned white. "I can't wait to get it off my chest, you know? I thought it would be too hard if I told her on the phone, or in an e-mail. I don't want her to think it's more than it is."

"Definitely," Jacqui agreed. She was relieved Eliza was finally going to come clean. Eliza had been adamant about keeping the Big Palm Beach Secret a secret, so Jacqui had reluctantly promised not to tell Mara, and as a result Jacqui hadn't talked to Mara since before New Year's. Jacqui didn't want to lie to her, and with the studying and the time difference, it hadn't been that hard to fall out of touch.

"Anyway, tell me more about this new job of yours," Jacqui said, changing the subject since Eliza looked so uncomfortable. "Are you really going to get to meet all those stars?"

Eliza happily obliged, and the two forgot all about Palm Beach as they gossiped and chatted all the way to the East Hampton airport. The airport was a remote field off the dirt roads, and when they arrived, they found Mara in the middle of a crowd, kissing several well-heeled people good-bye. Eliza recognized a few of the socialites gathered around her and was impressed. But then, after Mara had merited not one but three glowing profiles in the Hamptons media last summer, Eliza hadn't expected anything less from her friend. Whether she'd planned on it or not, Mara was Somebody in the Hamptons.

Eliza leaned on the horn. "Over here!" She threw open the car door and climbed out, and Jacqui followed suit. They were both excited to see Mara—the three of them hadn't been together since last August, and they were eager to pick up where they'd left off.

Mara's eyes lit up and she quickly rushed over to Eliza and Jacqui. "Hello! Hello!" she enthused, embracing Eliza warmly. "I've missed you guys!" she said, giving Jacqui a similar bear hug. "You both look amazing!"

The cooing and the fawning began anew, as Eliza and Jacqui marveled over Mara's highlights, and Mara praised them on their tans and cute outfits.

"God, I can't believe I'm back. It's like I never left!" Mara shook her head and hiccuped.

"Mara, are you tipsy?" Eliza asked. Last summer, Mara had been such a goody-goody they'd practically had to drag her out to parties.

"A little," Mara giggled. "I had a little—*hiccup*—Cristal on the plane."

Jacqui raised an eyebrow in admiration. Private plane, five-hundred-dollar champagne—this girl knew how to roll.

The three of them grinned at each other, remembering how much fun last summer had been, and wondering what kind of mischief and adventure lay ahead for them this time. Everything was lush and green after the rainstorm, and the air smelled like salt and earth, mixed with a wonderful woodsy scent. All three girls felt lucky to be alive, in the Hamptons, and finally back together.

Mara stuffed her bag in the trunk, then opened the back door. "Er . . ." she said, not quite sure where to sit. The backseat of Eliza's car was akin to a homeless person's grocery cart. It was filled to the brim with empty water bottles, torn shopping bags, shoe boxes, CDs, Advantage bar wrappers, and carb-free tortilla chip bags. It was odd how someone as perfect-looking as Eliza, who was such a neat freak about her clothes, hair, and person, had turned her car into what was essentially a dump truck. It was one of the things that Mara liked so much about her—you could never pin Eliza down to a stereotype.

"Eek. Sorry about the mess," Eliza apologized sheepishly.

Mara grinned and pushed aside Eliza's dry cleaning so she could sit down.

"Anybody hungry?" Mara asked. "They had these, like,

imported Majorcan almonds on board—they had so many, I took a couple of bags. Here, have some. They're yummy."

Eliza started the car and Mara handed out her pilfered snacks.

"So spill! How was Palm Beach? You guys never told me what happened!" Mara demanded. She was still giddy and high from the plane ride. Garrett had been a total ham the entire trip, and at one point, he'd turned the plane into a flying disco and had whirled Mara around until she was dizzy. Her good mood was so contagious that Jacqui momentarily forgot that Palm Beach was dangerous territory.

"It was fun!" Jacqui said. "We got to borrow these couture ball gowns for the twins' debut, I wore a Lacroix with a hand-beaded corset that Poppy didn't want, and Eliza got this amazing Chanel dress that Karl had made for Sugar."

Mara oohed and aahed at Jacqui's description of the house and the New Year's Eve party, and Eliza knew this was the moment she'd have to tell her best friend what exactly had happened with her best friend's ex-boyfriend. "Mar, I have something really important to tell you about Palm Beach. . . ."

Mara looked at Eliza expectantly. If she felt a twinge of foreboding, she didn't reveal it. Her face was wide open and innocent.

Jacqui held her breath. She'd put Eliza and Ryan's hookup out of her mind for a second, but looking back and forth between her two friends, she knew that what was about to happen would be totally unforgettable.

the girls meet the perrys' latest french import

"HOLD UP!" MARA SAID, INTERRUPTING ELIZA. AN OLD Madonna song came on the radio, and Mara leaned through the front seats to turn it up.

" 'Papa don't preach!' " they all sang. " 'I'm in trouble deep!' "

Mara thought she couldn't be happier. It was great to be back with Eliza and Jacqui in the Hamptons again. She'd really missed them. There was no one as fun as Eliza or as mischievous as Jacqui back home.

The song ended, but before Eliza could speak, Mara suddenly blurted, "God, I just can't wait to see Ryan!"

"Really?" Jacqui asked. "Even after you broke up with him?"

"I know, I know." Mara sighed. Her champagne buzz was still strong. "You guys, I really think I made a mistake. I mean, he said he still loved me, you know, even after I said we couldn't go on, and I just hope . . . I don't know. . . . Do you know if he's see-ing anyone?" Mara asked hopefully.

Eliza cleared her throat. If she was going to tell, she would have to do it now, before this got even worse. It was obvious Mara was still in love with Ryan, and the knowledge that he had hooked up with one of her friends was bound to be crushing. Best to get it over with quickly. Mara would be upset, but she would understand and hopefully forgive Eliza.

"Mar, listen, this is important. Please don't be mad at me, okay? Because it meant nothing, I *swear*. This winter in Palm Beach I—"

"That's the thing," Mara said, interrupting again, obviously oblivious to the rising notes of anxiety in Eliza's voice. "I wish I'd gone to Palm Beach. God, I don't know why I stayed away. I just . . . I really regret it. I should have listened to you, Jac."

Jacqui stayed silent.

"Anyway, what did you want to tell me, 'Liza? Why shouldn't I be mad?" Mara asked, starting to braid Eliza's hair, which was hanging over the back of her seat. "What happened in Palm Beach?"

Eliza sucked her teeth. "Over winter break I . . . I . . ." Eliza felt her throat dry up. She exhaled. "I decided not to work for the Perrys this summer. I'm not going to be an au pair."

"*What?!*" Mara and Jacqui both said, shocked for very different reasons.

Eliza gnawed on her bottom lip. She'd meant to tell Mara— really she had. She'd been going to confess everything and get it over with. Mara was different from Lindsay and Taylor, those two-faced former best friends who'd turned on Eliza last year.

Eliza always felt like she could tell Mara anything. Okay, so maybe they hadn't kept in touch all that much over the school year, but that was irrelevant, Eliza almost felt like the year apart hadn't even happened.

Eliza shrugged her shoulders helplessly at Jacqui. She knew Jacqui would think she was a coward and a liar. She could live with that, but she couldn't live with Mara's disappointment. She was just too scared to hurt her friend. Besides, she reasoned, maybe keeping her mouth shut was the best option. That way, Mara and Ryan could get back together without having any bad feelings between them. If Eliza ignored the problem, then it would surely just go away, right?

"What are you doing, then?" Mara asked, interrupting Eliza's internal debate.

"I'm working at Seventh Circle, this new nightclub," Eliza said proudly. "It's really cool—I'll be learning all about public relations and stuff. I don't really need the money from the Perrys this summer. My dad's doing better, and we might even move back to the city next year."

Mara slumped in the backseat. "Jac, you knew about this?"

Jacqui nodded.

"And you didn't tell me?" Mara whined.

"I'm sorry—I thought Eliza e-mailed you." Jacqui shot Eliza another daggerlike look. Then again, if Mara was this upset about not knowing about Eliza's summer plans, Jacqui was kind of glad she hadn't told her about Palm Beach.

"That's great and all," Mara said. "I mean, I'm really happy for you 'Lize. But what are we going to do without you? Who's going to scare William into submission? Are we ever going to see you?"

"What are you talking about? We'll see each other all the time," Eliza promised.

Eliza turned into the Perry driveway, where several expensive cars were parked. The newest addition to the fleet was a shiny new Toyota Prius, a gas/electric hybrid car that was the latest Hamptons automobile obsession. Priuses were politically correct, environmentally friendly, and incredibly hard to find—there was a six-month waiting list, and cars were selling for fifty percent over sticker price. Next to the Prius was Ryan Perry's Aston Martin. But since Ryan was a touchy subject, nobody said anything.

Laurie, Anna Perry's personal assistant, a frowsy-haired forty-year-old woman who wore a cell phone around her neck on a leash and lived vicariously through her employers, greeted them at the front door.

"Girls! Welcome back! Eliza, what are you doing here? Anna and the kids arrive tomorrow morning from the city. They were supposed to come in today, but Kevin needed the heli for some emergency meeting in Connecticut, and Anna didn't want to sit in traffic. Ryan and the twins are around somewhere. Jacqui, Mara, you have the night off after getting the kids' rooms ready."

They all followed Laurie inside and found the Perry house

the same as ever, with immense floral arrangements in every corner, the striped zebrawood floors polished to a high sheen, every
room perfectly appointed and camera-ready for an *Architectural
Digest* shoot. Laurie told them that the Perrys paid a skeleton
staff to keep the house looking this way even in the dead of winter. It was important that the house be prepared for their arrival
at any moment, even if months passed between visits during the
off-season.

"What's that noise?" Mara asked. "Is that a cement mixer?"
Her father was in construction, and she recognized the sound.

Laurie grimaced and put her hands to her ears. "It's the
Reynolds Castle. They're not supposed to have construction after
five. I've already told Anna we should report it to city hall."

The three girls scurried to the picture window and spied a
humongous structure being built over a traditional Victorian
house. The sprawling wood skeleton, complete with turrets, tow-
ers, and what looked like a moat, seemed to span the entire
length of the property, all the way down to the beachfront. A
huge crane was lifting up several gold-plated Grecian columns.
They stared, fascinated, as a forty-foot-wide stained glass cathe-
dral window was positioned on the top floor.

"It's a shame what they're doing to the old Rockefeller place,"
Laurie sniffed, as insulted as a true East Hampton blueblood. "It's
a monstrosity!"

"Here, I'll help you guys with your things," Eliza said, grab-
bing Jacqui's makeup bag and Mara's magazines.

The girls walked through the kitchen to the back door that led out to the terrace and garden. The grounds were pristine, the croquet set laid out for a game, and in the distance, the tennis and basketball courts shone with new paint.

"Oh my God. Who is that?" Eliza asked in a stage whisper, when they reached the pool patio.

Lounging on a raft in the middle of the infinity pool was the most beautiful boy they had ever seen. His entire lean, bronzed body was caramel-colored, from his honey-blond hair to his nut-brown tan. A cigarette dangled from his lower lip. He was wearing aviator sunglasses and holding a frosted cocktail glass with an umbrella in it.

"*Bonjour,*" the beautiful boy drawled, trailing a finger on the water.

Jacqui's chest heaved. Had she said, "No more boys"? Did it count if he was the most gorgeous creature she had ever seen?

He raised his sunglasses to appraise them, a playful smile on his lips.

"Hi," Mara said weakly.

"*Bonjour* yourself," Eliza shot back.

"*Boa tarde.*" Jacqui smiled.

"*Je m'appelle* Philippe Dufourg. You must be my coworkers, two of you at least," he said, in a sexy French accent.

"Coworker?" Mara asked. "You're not . . ."

He grinned, puffing on his cigarette and flicking his ashes into the chlorine-blue waters. "*Mais oui.* I am the new au pair."

aren't rules made to be broken?

LAURIE FILLED THEM IN AS SHE LED THEM TO THE SERVANTS' cottage—Philippe was the French nephew of the kids' regular nanny, who took every summer off to go home to Cornwall. He went to school in London—hence the (almost) perfect English— and had arrived just that morning. Philippe was an aspiring tennis pro and hoped to bolster his reputation by winning the Rolex Invitational, which took place in East Hampton each July. Besides babysitting the children, he was going to give them private tennis lessons.

"And as you can see, he's made himself quite at home," Laurie said, with a hint of disapproval. "Well, here you are," she said, throwing open the door to the tidy cottage.

Everything was exactly as they remembered it. Even the third step on the rickety stairs still squeaked. Their room was as plain and bare as a prison cell, but they hadn't expected anything more. There were a bunk bed and a small single bed, each with one flat pillow and scratchy wool blankets. Against the opposite wall were

43

two bureaus, a ratty armchair, and a nightstand with a lamp that didn't work that well ever since Eliza had tripped on its wire one night last July. There was one new addition, though: a shiny white intercom/phone, which Laurie explained Anna had had installed so they could get in touch with the au pairs with the push of a button.

Mara and Jacqui began unpacking, chattering about this exciting new development (the boy, not the phone) as they decided on drawers and beds. "Do you want the top bunk?" Mara asked Jacqui.

"Sure. Thanks. Where do you think they put the boy?" Jacqui nodded, pulling aside the curtain on the one small attic window.

Mara shrugged. She hadn't given Philippe a second thought—she was still fixated on the Aston Martin, wondering if Ryan was on the grounds somewhere. Maybe he was in his room, or in the kitchen. Maybe she should do a little scouting. . . .

Eliza sat on the single bed, feeling a little out of place. She felt nostalgic for last summer, remembering all the wild times they'd shared together in this small space—sneaking smokes out the window and bottles of Grey Goose from the Perrys' liquor cabinet. She and Jeremy had first made out on the very bed she was sitting on. But the feeling ended when she spotted a row of dust bunnies underneath the nightstand and remembered her air-conditioned bedroom back at her family's summer rental.

"Hey—that's a nice necklace. Ryan has one just like it, doesn't he?" Mara asked, looking up from unpacking and noticing the leather string Eliza was holding between her fingers, lost in thought.

"Oh!" Eliza's hands flew from her neck. She looked around nervously. "Yeah. It's nothing, just this old thing I picked up."

"Did you guys hang out in Florida?" Mara asked wistfully. "You and Ryan? How was he?"

Eliza colored. "Excuse me?"

"I dunno, what did he look like? Was he with anyone?" Mara asked.

"Same as always," Eliza shrugged. "He wasn't around much. Anyway, what about that guy by the pool, huh? How lucky are you guys? What a hottie!" she said, to change the subject. She motioned to the two of them to come closer. "I heard French guys have the biggest . . ."

Jacqui and Mara giggled.

Just then, Philippe walked in, smelling of smoke and coconut suntan oil. Jacqui thought nothing smelled sexier. "*Bon!*" he said, rubbing his palms together. "*Ça devrait être amusant, trois filles et moi!*"

"No way, you're not staying *here*, are you?" Mara asked, realizing he was saying something about his room. Anna didn't seriously think to put two girls and one very hot guy in the same room, did she? But then, Anna Perry wasn't really one for propriety. Mara was aghast.

Jacqui shrugged. What was the big deal? Obviously Mara had never backpacked through Europe. She was intrigued.

45

Philippe was staying in the same room with them. How very . . . convenient.

"*Oui*." Philippe nodded. He rummaged in the top bureau drawer for a shirt and pants and began to peel off his trunks.

"Hold it! What do you think you're doing?" Mara demanded. She knew she was being a killjoy, but seriously, this was out of line. She didn't care if he *was* hot and French—she didn't want to feel awkward around him all summer. He would have to learn how to respect her privacy, even if he had no need for his own.

Eliza and Jacqui looked a little disappointed. That little slice of Philippe's perfect backside was tantalizing. They had been looking forward to the show.

Philippe shrugged. "Nakedness is not allowed? But I am in my room?"

Eliza and Jacqui watched, amused, as Mara marched Philippe to the hallway, holding his arms firmly to his sides. Now this was the uptight Mara they remembered. "In America, we change in private!" Mara insisted.

Mara walked back into the room, wiping her palms in consternation. "Can you believe that guy? Anyway, Jac, I guess he gets that drawer next to the bed. Huh. Well, do you want to share that closet then? And I guess we should see what Laurie needs us to do."

"Yeah—I guess I should go . . ." Eliza said awkwardly, standing up and collecting her purse. It was weird to be back in the old room and not be able to stay. "Hey, what are you guys doing tomorrow night? Do you want to come over to my house and hang out? I don't start work till Saturday."

"Maybe," Jacqui said, realizing for the second time in only a few minutes that her plan to ignore all distractions and be a stellar babysitter was not going to be as easy as she'd hoped. "If we can put the kids to bed early."

"Don't worry, we'll be there," Mara assured her. If there was one thing Mara had learned last year, it was that they could figure out a way to take care of the kids *and* have a good time.

Eliza raised an eyebrow and smiled. Jacqui being responsible? Mara ready to party? Some things really did change. They hugged Eliza good-bye, promising to call her soon.

When Eliza left, her slides click-clacking loudly on the stairs, Philippe reentered the room, looking freshly shaven and wearing a starched white oxford shirt and perfectly pressed blue jeans.

"Better?" he asked Mara.

Mara nodded coolly. She had finished putting away all of her clothes, not having brought as many as Jacqui, who had already crammed the closet with her wardrobe. "I'm going to see what Laurie needs for the kids' rooms."

"I'll be there in a bit," Jacqui promised, not meeting Mara's eyes. She was fully conscious that Philippe had sprawled, emperor-like, on the single bed and was staring at her expectantly.

Mara shrugged her shoulders and left, thinking she might take a few unnecessary detours on the way to Laurie's office—say, the landing right by Ryan's room.

"So, Jacqui, are you also needing to see Laurie?" Philippe asked Jacqui. "Because there are still some, what you call it, piña coladas in the blender."

Jacqui stopped putting her clothes away. She knew that the right thing to do was to follow Mara and get everything prepared for the kids tomorrow. But Philippe was still smiling at her, a dazzling preponderance of shiny white teeth and blue eyes. He reached under the bed and brought out a half-empty bottle of Bacardi. "Help me finish this?" he asked.

"I guess I am kind of thirsty . . ." Jacqui allowed. She had sworn to herself that she was really going to be better this summer: she was going to keep her head down, she was going to help Mara take care of the kids, she was going to study for that uh, test thing, S-A . . . whatever was it called again. . . .

She exhaled loudly, squaring her shoulders, and looked straight into his eyes. "But you know what? I think I'll just catch up with you later," she told Philippe, running out of the room before he could say her name again in that sexy accent of his.

reunited, and it feels
so . . . awkward

MARA WOKE UP EARLY THEIR FIRST DAY IN THE AU PAIRS'
room, tossing off the sheets and yawning. Jacqui was snoozing on
the top bunk, and Philippe was snoring loudly under a mountain
of blankets on the single bed. Last night, she and Jacqui had
returned to the room to find Philippe smoking cigarettes and
playing solitaire card games by himself. They'd joined him for a
few hands of hearts before turning in early.

Mara had spent most of yesterday evening skulking around
the main house, hoping to catch Ryan, without any luck.
Knowing he always got up early to surf before breakfast, she'd set
the alarm and hoped to catch him on his way out. She was extra-
careful to put on a cute outfit—a pale-green shrunken T-shirt
that showed off her small waist, and Jessica Simpson–like cutoff
jean shorts that showed off her legs. She put her long brown hair
in a messy ponytail, taking care to frame a few loose tendrils
around her face.

Unfortunately, there was no sign of Ryan in his wet suit

checking the weather on the flat-screen TV in the kitchen, or waxing down his board in the driveway. Mara stared at the parked Aston Martin, as if willing Ryan to appear. Her shoulders slumped as she walked back into the house, wondering if he was avoiding her. Back in the kitchen, she helped herself to a cup of yogurt and heard voices coming from the patio. Her stomach clenched out of nervousness, and she opened the sliding door.

Ryan was standing on the terrace, talking to a tall, blond girl. He looked up, startled, when he saw Mara. He was wearing a hooded sweatshirt and faded jeans, and was holding a sleeping bag under one arm and an Igloo cooler in the other. His hair was comically tousled, sticking out in every direction, and he had pillow creases on his cheek, but they only made him look more adorable. As usual, he was barefoot, and his toes were covered with sand.

"Hey!" he said, and for an instant, Mara caught a glimpse of his open, dimpled smile, but it soon vanished into an embarrassed grimace. "Mara—I didn't know you were here."

"I got in yesterday," she said, forcing a light tone. *Who the hell was this girl?* "Sorry for interrupting."

Ryan dropped his things and walked toward her, his arms extended. "Not at all. It's great to see you," he said, making sure not to make contact with any part of her body other than her back, which he thumped as if she were one of his soccer teammates. She smelled the saltwater in his hair, which reminded her painfully of last summer.

"You too," she said, finding it difficult to breathe.

He was even more gorgeous than she'd remembered. The sun had lightened his hair, and his green eyes sparkled in his darkly tanned face. He moved with the same easy grace, projected the same laid-back, down-to-earth vibe. The kind of guy who'd been born with everything and hadn't let that happy accident spoil him one bit. Mara had always thought he was way out of her league—but for one week last summer, he'd been blessedly, deliciously, gloriously hers. And now she wanted him back.

"Allison was just giving me a ride home," Ryan explained, introducing the girls to each other. "Remember my friend Oz? He had a bonfire last night," he said, looping his arm around the six-foot-tall Charlize Theron clone. Allison was wearing a thin white tank top and drawstring pajamas. Her hair was messy and uncombed, but Mara noted how effortlessly sexy she looked. This was not a girl who took half an hour choosing just the right outfit and pulling tendrils out of her ponytail.

"And this one was in no condition to drive!" Allison cooed, tickling Ryan's stomach.

"Hey!" Ryan protested, smacking her hands away. They wrestled, and Allison pretended to get upset when Ryan caught her hands behind her back.

Mara watched them flirt, her stomach tightening. Just a year ago she and Ryan had spent almost every night of the last week entwined in each other's arms and telling each other their deepest, darkest secrets. She remembered every scar on his body (the

51

one from when he blasted his knee skiing, the one down the side of his right calf from wiping out on his skateboard), every story he'd told her about growing up (Christmases in Maine, his Outward Bound safari in Kenya, how he still had lunch with his old Latin professor in New York), and especially the way his nose crinkled when he closed his eyes and kissed her. Even though Mara knew she was the one who'd broken up with him, it hurt to see him flirt with someone else.

Mara was relieved when the show was over, but felt anxious when Ryan took a seat next to her on the patio table. Allison mentioned something about being cold, and Mara watched the girl's long, lithe figure glide to where a jeep was parked on the sand. They had driven up the back way, onto the private beach-front that bordered the Perry estate, which meant that Allison came from a family that also owned a mansion on Georgica, since the back roads were all private. Allison was exactly the kind of girl a guy like Ryan Perry was meant to be with. Mara put down her yogurt cup; she'd lost her appetite.

Allison bounded back up to the patio, wearing a boy-sized Dartmouth sweatshirt. Mara remembered that Ryan had wanted to go to Dartmouth and wondered if he'd gotten in. Allison promptly sat on Ryan's lap.

"What's this?" Allison asked, poking at an exotic-looking fruit display in the middle of the table.

"That's a persimmon," Ryan said, pointing to what looked like a squashed orange tomato. "And this is a rambutan," he explained, holding up a prickly red ball. "Anna gets them shipped in from Indonesia."

One of Anna's many pretensions was snobbery over the local produce. Even if the Hamptons were famous for their plump strawberries, peaches, and pears, rare, expensive and imported always trumped fresh and available.

"How do I open this?" Allison asked.

Ryan showed her how to delicately peel the skin, exposing the white jellylike substance inside.

"Yum!" Allison said, chewing. She peeled another and fed it to Ryan, who rewarded her with a kiss. They laughed and giggled, and Mara felt like she might vomit. She slid her chair back to get up.

"So, how was the Jitney? Crowded?" Ryan asked, finally looking in her direction.

She shook her head. "No—I flew. Anna set it up so I could ride with the Reynoldses on their jet."

"Really?" Allison interjected. "What's it like? I heard it's so tacky!" she said, her eyes wide.

"It's a new G5," Mara retorted, remembering what Garret had told her about the plane. "It's actually really nice," she added, feeling defensive.

"I bet," Ryan said, and Mara thought she heard a bite in his tone.

"Garrett is really sweet. He said he knows you," Mara said, deciding to feel Ryan out.

"He used to be a good friend of mine," Ryan said, his face stony. "But he's not anymore."

Just then, a piercing whistle interrupted the early-morning silence, and they looked up to see the object of their conversation standing in front of the dirt path between the two houses, holding up a tennis ball. "Bounced over the fence," Garrett Reynolds explained. He was wearing crisp tennis whites and looked like a Ralph Lauren model.

"Hey," Ryan grunted.

"Hi, Gar," Allison cooed. "Heard you guys got some new wings."

Garrett nodded, smiling. He shambled over, pointing a finger at Mara. "Hi, gorgeous. We on for tomorrow night? I hope you've changed your mind. I've got the best table at the American reserved."

Just yesterday, Mara had gently turned him down for a date, but after the display Ryan had just put on with Allison, she decided to change course. Mara smiled winningly back at Garrett. "Sure, why not?" she told him.

"Good girl. Pick you up at seven." Garrett grinned. "'Bye, Ali. Later, Perry," he told Ryan, bouncing the tennis ball on his racket as he disappeared behind the hedges.

Ryan cleared his throat. "Well. Have fun tomorrow night," he said brusquely. "By the way, I think Laurie's in her office," he said, talking to Mara as if she was just one of the many people who worked for the Perrys. He turned back to Allison, helping her up from her seat, and the two of them disappeared into the house.

Everything Mara had been hoping for—getting back together with Ryan, the two of them picking up exactly where they'd left off—was dashed before the summer had even begun. But before she could sink any further into her sadness, the ground suddenly began to shake, and Mara looked out to see a silver helicopter land on the lawn, whipping the tall grass to the ground.

An emaciated woman wearing a billowing African muumuu stepped gingerly out of the side door, futilely shielding her hairdo against the wind and yelling at the copilots. Several children tumbled out after her, screaming loudly for their breakfast.

Anna Perry and the Perry kids had finally arrived.

the perry kids have a lot to learn, and medication to take

ANNA PERRY SAT IN FRONT OF THE GAMING TABLE in the Perrys' state-of-the-art screening room, drumming her fingers against the green felt. Next to her sat Laurie, her fingers poised on a laptop computer. The sixteen-foot-wide projection screen in the front of the room showed a colorful PowerPoint presentation page that displayed PERRY CHILDREN SUMMER GOALS in marquee lettering.

Mara sat across from them, pensive and tense after the early-morning encounter with Ryan and his new girlfriend. Next to her were two empty chairs. Jacqui and Philippe were late. A bearded, bespectacled gentleman in a shabby tweed suit, holding a notebook, sat on Anna's left. Mara wondered who he was.

A slim eleven-year-old girl walked in, a skinny teen Mara had spied leaving the helicopter earlier. She hadn't recognized the girl from far away, but now she could see that she was someone very familiar indeed.

"Madison!" Mara called. "Hi, sweetie!"

The newly svelte Madison allowed Mara a cool nod. Last summer, Mara had been Madison's champion, defending her against a mean ballet teacher and bucking her up when William teased her. Mara attempted a hug, but Madison stood out of arm's reach.

"Anna, do you like this shirt on me?" Madison asked, turning to whisper in Anna's ear. The little girl with curly hair who favored oversized T-shirts and shorts had grown up to become a Jamie Lynn Spears clone with flat-ironed locks, wearing bootleg jeans and a tight tank top that showed off her midriff.

A few minutes later, Madison kissed the air next to Anna's cheek and pranced out the door, just as Jacqui rushed in, her hair wet, followed closely by Philippe. The two of them seemed to be sharing some secret joke, and Mara noticed Anna's lips pucker at the sight of them.

"Philippe! *Vous vous êtes bien installé?*" Anna said graciously in a perfect French accent.

"*Oui, madame, il est très beau ici,*" he said, giving her the full benefit of his smile.

Anna glowed. "Well, Kevin and I are so glad to have everyone here for the summer," she said grandly. "I take it, Jacqui and Mara, you've met Philippe. Philippe, Jacqui and Mara have worked for us before, so they can fill you in if I forget to mention anything. This will be very short, as I have a committee meeting at the Parrish in a few minutes." Anna was forever dropping names and making allusions to various nabobs of Hamptons society, which always went over the heads of the au pairs.

"First, let me introduce you to Dr. Pell Abraham, William's new therapist. Dr. Abraham will be monitoring William for his hyperactivity disorder. Jacqui, I don't need to remind you what happened in Palm Beach. Needless to say, we can't have that happen again. My scars have disappeared with laser therapy, thank God. Laurie, can we have the lights, please?" Anna asked. "First slide. Thank you," she said, as the PowerPoint page gave way to a screen showing a photo of William sticking his tongue out, next to a bullet-pointed list of his "issues." At Anna's direction, Laurie had put together a PowerPoint presentation on the Perry children, as neatly organized and soullessly rendered as a corporate sales pitch.

"As you can all see, we're hoping to send William to Eton next year, and they won't accept him if he fails to qualify due to his mental illness," Anna said, using a laser pointer to highlight the words *ADHD disorder—new prescriptions*. "Dr. Abraham will be conducting experiments and focusing on how William's family life affects his condition. Please don't mind him as he sits in on activities or asks questions."

Mara blanched. Not only was Anna getting rid of the kid, she was sending him clear across the ocean. Eton was an elite English boarding school that counted the future king of England as an alumnus. Anna had found a way to further her social-climbing aspirations as well as divest herself of her most difficult stepchild. Worse yet, this summer there was going to be some weird doctor following him around and taking notes. That should do *wonders* for William's behavioral problems.

Laurie clicked the remote, and Zoë's screen came up. "We think it would be wonderful if Zoë learned to speak another language this year. Kevin and I were so pleased when she started reading that Portuguese children's book last summer. But we think she should really branch out to a more . . . ah, historically and culturally rich language. Something a little more challenging. We've chosen Russian. I studied Chekhov in college, and I think it will be wonderful for her to get a head start on the classics."

A seven-year-old studying Russian? How were they going to manage that? Mara had barely passed Spanish. It was just like Anna to choose a language that neither of the foreign-born au pairs spoke.

"As for Cody, Dr. Abraham has alerted me to the fact that he has begun to exhibit warning signs that hint of a borderline personality. So he will also have to be monitored very closely."

Jacqui took copious notes, which Mara had to snigger at, while Philippe put his hands behind his head and kicked his chair back. He yawned openly.

The slide clicked, showing a weekly calendar.

"We've decided on a very packed schedule for them this

summer. Idle hands, idle minds, the devil's playground, and all that. Sundays and Mondays are surfing in Montauk, Tuesdays are music and art appreciation, horseback riding on Wednesdays, kabala camp on Thursdays, and etiquette and ballroom dancing at the country club on Fridays. Saturdays they can do as they please, but I hope you can encourage the children to do something productive, like practice their meditation. Spirituality is so important." Anna nodded to Laurie and the lights flashed back on.

"Excuse me, Anna, what about Madison? Do we have any goals for her this summer?" Mara asked.

"Madison is eleven. Too old to have an au pair anymore," Anna said. "No need to worry about her. We're so proud that she finally found success with her new diet!"

The rest of the day was a manic blur, and when the kids were safely tucked into bed, Mara and Jacqui returned, exhausted, to their room. Philippe had skipped out soon after the first disastrous tennis lesson. (William had used his racquet as a blunt instrument, Zoë swung hers like a baseball bat, and Cody could barely lift his.)

"I'm so tired!" Jacqui said, heaving herself up with difficulty onto the top bunk. "I don't remember last summer being this much work!"

Mara's mouth opened with a ready reply, but when she saw Jacqui's face, she burst out laughing. At least Jacqui was around to lend a hand this time—who even knew where Philippe had gone?

They'd barely had a chance to relax when the new phone began to ring.

"Au pairs!" Mara answered, just as Anna had instructed them, even though it made her feel silly.

"No kidding," Eliza guffawed. "You bitches coming over or what?" she demanded. "My parents just left for the night and I just found a great mojito recipe. Bring mint!"

when skinny-dipping
at night, it helps
to get sloshed

WHEN THEY ARRIVED AT ELIZA'S HOUSE, IT WAS ALMOST ten o'clock in the evening, since Jacqui had insisted on trying to find Philippe to invite him to come along. "It seems rude to just leave him here," Jacqui told Mara. Even though she'd promised herself no more boys, there was nothing wrong with being friendly, was there? But the French boy never resurfaced, and Mara, who was tired of waiting, persuaded Jacqui to leave him a note with directions to the Thompsons' house instead. The only car left in the driveway was Ryan's Aston Martin, and even though the Perrys had always assured them they could use any car in the lot that was available, they decided to hitch a ride to Westhampton with one of the day staff instead. They figured they could call a taxi or something for the ride back.

The Thompsons' rental was a weathered New England cottage with an inviting wraparound porch. It was nestled in a pretty cul-de-sac and shaded by a grove of bent oak trees. Several single-passenger kayaks and long wooden paddles were stacked on its front lawn.

Eliza greeted them at the door with a tray of frosty mojitos in tall glasses.

"About time," she chided, handing out drinks. "I thought I'd have to drink these all myself."

Eliza gave Jacqui and Mara a quick tour. "I don't think they've renovated since the seventies," she sighed, shaking her head at the orange shag rug. "And of course, we're on the wrong side of the highway," she added, since the house was located north of Route 27.

Mara looked around admiringly. She really couldn't understand Eliza sometimes. Sure, it was nothing like the Perrys' designer show palace on Georgica, but it was airy and comfortable nonetheless. While the house looked small from the outside, Mara counted six bedrooms—two in the attic, three on the ground floor, and one downstairs in the expansive finished basement, complete with a dartboard and a foosball table. Eliza had no idea how good she had it.

They made their way to the back patio, where Eliza pointed out the "crummy" pool and the "gross" hot tub. The three of them sat at the edge of the pool and let their legs dangle over the side, balancing their drinks carefully.

"This is delish," Mara said, taking a big gulp from her glass, careful not to splash on her shirt. The sugarcane and mint mixed with the rum had a pleasant salty but sweet taste.

"Mmm," Jacqui agreed. God, it was heaven to be away from those kids. She borrowed a cigarette from Eliza's pack. Eliza lit one too and offered Mara one. After shaking her head, Mara changed her mind and took one as well. They puffed contentedly, sipping their drinks.

Eliza asked them about their day and listened keenly as Mara described her disappointment at finding Ryan involved with someone else so soon.

"I know Allison Evans," Eliza said carefully, keeping her voice even. "I didn't know they were together. Are you sure? Because Ryan has lots of girlfriends—I mean, friends who are girls," she said a little awkwardly, thinking of how she was one of Ryan's "friends who are girls" as well. "Maybe you should ask him about it?"

Mara shrugged. "What's the point? He totally acted like I was nothing to him." She drained her glass, feeling the effects of the rum. "I should have known."

Jacqui put her arm around Mara's shoulder in sympathy and gave her a squeeze. "It's okay, *chica*, everyone makes mistakes," Jacqui said as she looked at Eliza meaningfully. If Eliza was ever going to own up to Palm Beach, this was the perfect time to do it.

But Eliza didn't meet Jacqui's gaze. "Look at it this way, Mar, at least you know you're not going to die a virgin," she said ruefully, stubbing out her cigarette on the tile.

"You and Jeremy never—?" Mara asked.

"Dating long-distance didn't really work for us." Eliza sighed. "He's supposed to stop by the club tomorrow. But I don't know. . . .

I'm afraid he might be seeing someone else too," she lamented. Jeremy had finally returned her call yesterday. He'd said he was really looking forward to seeing her, but he'd been curt and distracted on the phone.

"With my track record, I'll probably never get to do it. Something *always* happens. I'm just trying to give it away, and no one will take me up on it!" Eliza whined, fully aware of how ridiculous she sounded.

"Here lies Eliza Marie Thompson," Jacqui said in a grave tone. "The Last American Virgin. She tried to give it away, but no one would take it. May she rest in peace."

Jacqui and Mara giggled. Eliza pretended to be insulted and then gave in to the laughter bubbling up inside of her.

"C'mon," she said, dragging them up to their feet when their giggles subsided. She was suddenly energized with a new plan. She grabbed the bottle of rum. Screw dangling their feet in this dinky little washbasin—the ocean wasn't far.

To get there faster, they cut through the neighbors' yards diagonally, ducking under clotheslines and stepping over kids' go-carts until they reached the shore. They watched the waves rumble in, cresting on the horizon. The cool night air smelled damp and salty. Eliza stuck a toe in the water. "It's warm," she marveled. The Atlantic was *never* warm. The waters off Long Island usually felt like an ice bath, especially in the evening. In Eliza's buzzed state, she decided it must be a sign. "Let's go swimming!" she said, exhilarated.

"Hello, we're not wearing bathing suits," Mara protested, wading into the shallows. The water *was* comfortably temperate, but still . . .

"So what?" Eliza shrugged, already tossing off her cardigan. She felt hot from all the rum. A dunk in the ocean sounded like the perfect way to cool off.

Jacqui held her glass and assessed the situation. The water felt wonderful on her bare feet. She finished her drink and followed Eliza's lead, stepping out of her cotton sundress. She rarely wore any underwear anyway, and she ran laughing into the waves.

Eliza shed her T-shirt and capris, then quickly removed her bra and underwear as well. She whooped as she caught up to Jacqui in the water.

Jacqui and Eliza splashed around happily, calling to Mara. "C'mon, Mar! Or do you only swim naked with boys?" Eliza called teasingly, reminding Mara that she'd been caught skinny-dipping with Ryan in the Perrys' pool last year—by her boyfriend, no less.

That did it. Mara unbuttoned her blouse and stepped out of her jeans. She hitched her camisole over her head and folded her underwear neatly on top of her clothes.

"Banzai!" Mara laughed, as she cartwheeled into the ocean.

They swam around lazily for a while, feeling delightfully wicked. This was what summer was all about! They floated on their backs and looked up at the stars and then took turns dunking each other. After a little while, the alcohol they'd drunk wore off and they all discovered the same thing, at just about the same time: *The water was freezing!*

"I'm c-c-c-cold!" Eliza said, shivering as she ran back to shore. She was in such a hurry to get back into her clothes, she put her shirt on backward. Mara and Jacqui followed, laughing at how stupid they'd been not to bring towels. They watched the waves roll in, and were about to head back, when Eliza was struck by an idea.

"Does anyone have a pen?" she asked, holding up the empty bottle of rum.

"I do," Mara said, fishing in her pocket and handing it to Eliza.

"What are you doing?" Jacqui asked, watching Eliza carefully peel away the label. Eliza smiled as she scribbled a few lines on the back of the label. She showed them what she had written, then folded it in thirds and stuck it inside the bottle. She screwed the cap back on, nice and tight.

"Did you ever do this as kids?" Eliza asked.

Jacqui and Mara shook their heads.

"It's fun. You never know who's going to get it," Eliza said. "Who's got the best arm? Mara?"

Mara shrugged and accepted the bottle. She threw it in a wide arc, and the three of them watched the bottle bob up and down until it disappeared into the waves. They trudged back to Eliza's house in good spirits.

"So you guys are coming tomorrow night to the club, right?

I'll put you on the list," Eliza said, as Jacqui flicked her cell open to call a taxi.

"Okay," Jacqui said slowly. She was already feeling worried about getting caught sneaking out tonight. "I guess it depends on when we get the kids to bed. . . ."

"Yeah, I don't know," Mara said. "I have this dinner thing earlier."

Eliza gripped Mara's shoulders affectionately, as if to shake away her doubts. "C'mon, it'll be fun. It's the first weekend of the summer. *Promise*."

"Is Ryan going to be there?" Mara asked, thinking she really didn't want a repeat of that morning again.

"So what if he is?" Eliza asked. "I mean, well, Mara—"

But suddenly, there was a flash of headlights as an Aston Martin Vanquish convertible turned into the driveway.

"*Bonjour!*" Philippe called out. Obviously, *he* had no qualms about using Ryan's car.

"Am I too late?" Philippe asked, a crooked smile on his lips when he saw how disheveled the girls were, their wet clothes plastered to their bodies.

"No, you're just in time," Jacqui replied briskly, "to drive us home."

anna perry is a lot younger than her botox implies

THE NEXT EVENING, AFTER WRESTLING THE KIDS TO bed, Jacqui walked into the playroom—a carpeted, windowless room in between the girls' and boys' bedrooms—and began putting away toys, games, skateboards, Legos, plastic pistols, Barbie dolls, and assorted talking stuffed animals in the plastic chest. The kids' wing was located in a remote, almost inaccessible corner of the house, behind a soundproofed door. Jacqui noticed that the kids couldn't have been farther from Anna's bedroom unless they were in the servants' cottage, but that a dual-level walk-in closet, complete with a built-in wet bar, was located right off the master bedroom.

Jacqui finished her task alone, since Mara was getting ready for her date with Garrett, and Philippe had wandered off again. But when she walked back to the cottage, she found Philippe sitting—no, *lounging* on the steps outside.

The lazy bastard. He was never around when they needed him. Jacqui put her hands on her hips, ready to give him a piece of her mind.

Seeing the look on her face, Philippe handed her a rolled-up joint. "Not really my scene," he explained, motioning back toward the house. "Here, take a *poof*."

It really wasn't a great idea to get stoned right on the property. Especially if she was concerned about getting a stellar reference from the Perrys at the end of the summer. But she was feeling a little tense . . . and, well, she wasn't one to turn down a hit. She accepted it and inhaled, feeling the acrid smoke hit the back of her throat.

"You are amazing," Philippe said. "*Ma tante* said it wouldn't be easy, but I did not think it would be this hard. I just wanted to be near the beach."

Jacqui laughed. She really couldn't be that angry at Philippe. He sounded just like she had last summer. They sat in companionable silence, listening to the crickets chirping in the bushes and watching the fireflies dance around the bushes by the pool. Philippe's cell phone rang a couple of times, but he ignored it.

"Who's trying to get hold of you so bad?" Jacqui asked when he ignored it the third time.

Philippe was nonchalant. "Just a couple of friends," he replied, and left it at that.

A few minutes later, Mara walked out of the door, wearing one of Jacqui's designer dresses. It was a low-cut Zac Posen lavender chiffon number, with beaded rhinestones that formed a pretty pattern on the neck and waist. The back dipped so low Mara was sure it was indecent, but Jacqui had assured her that none of the clothes Mara had brought would be dressy enough for dinner at the American Hotel.

Philippe whistled.

"I don't know if I put this on right," she said to Jacqui. "Does it look okay?"

Jacqui handed Philippe the roach, then stood up to judge. She pulled down on the waist, so that the neckline sat a little lower. "There. *Perfeito*. I have a pair of Jimmy Choo heels in my bag. Those are cute, but they're not high enough," Jacqui advised, pointing to Mara's sandals.

"What are you smoking?" Mara asked them, sniffing the fragrant air suspiciously.

"Nothing."

"*Rien.*"

Mara knew they were lying, but she was too concerned about looking presentable and too grateful to Jacqui for loaning her the dress to criticize them. Besides, she was tired of being the Good Girl all the time. Jacqui and Philippe were old enough to know the risks of getting fired if they were caught smoking pot.

"Tell Eliza I'm sorry I didn't make it, okay?" Mara told them, slipping on Jacqui's sandals. She walked up to the main house to wait for Garrett in the foyer.

Not long after Mara left, a pair of heels clicked on the concrete walk. Jacqui figured it was just Mara—she'd probably forgotten something—but it was Anna Perry who emerged from the darkness, dressed in a silk robe pulled tightly across her waist, and high-heeled brocade bedroom slippers. "I thought I smelled something," she said.

Jacqui choked on an exhale and tried to wave away the smoke.

"There you are," Anna said, smiling warmly at Philippe. "I was looking for you everywhere," she said flirtatiously, as Jacqui quickly hid the incriminating evidence behind her back.

"What are the two of you up to?" Anna asked, taking a seat next to Philippe by the curb. "Jacqui, is something wrong?"

Jacqui shook her head and surreptitiously threw down the joint, crushing it beneath her heel. "Nothing—we were just—nothing." Jacqui attempted a smile, edging away from the two of them. "I'm sorry, I'm really tired. I need to hit the straw. Um, good night!" she said, turning the doorknob to the servants' cottage.

She slammed the door behind her, her heart beating quickly in her chest. Her boss had busted them smoking pot! How would Anna ever recommend her for a job in New York now? Jacqui wondered what was going on outside, since Anna was still talking to Philippe. She pressed an ear to the door and found she could overhear parts of their conversation.

"Do you have anything?" she heard Anna ask.

Philippe murmured a protest.

"Don't be silly. I'm not that clueless, you know," Anna said.

Jacqui heard rustling and then Anna's voice again. "God, have I been craving this. Kevin is so boring sometimes. We used to have a lot of fun together, but now it's all just work, work, work."

Philippe snorted.

Jacqui couldn't believe it. Anna Perry! Smoking pot with one of the au pairs! Anna began to giggle at something Philippe said, and Jacqui suddenly felt abandoned, even though she was the one who'd left.

"How old do you think I am?" Anna asked Philippe.

Oh God, what an old line, Jacqui thought.

"Twenty-five," Philippe said graciously.

"Close, but no," Anna said. "I'm thirty-two. That's not too old, is it?"

Jacqui muffled a laugh. Thirty-two seemed kind of ancient to her.

"Sometimes I can't believe I'm thirty-two and the mother of seven children. Seven!" Anna shook her head. "I'm like Maria von Trapp or something."

Jacqui coughed. Anna was actually only the mother of one kid, Cody, and was a stepmom to the rest of the brood. Jacqui couldn't hear Philippe's reply. Then Anna said something about her life passing her by, and Jacqui realized the poor thing was lonely. It must suck not to have any real friends to talk to and to have to resort to the company of an employee. Still, why did it have to be Philippe?

After what seemed like an eternity, Jacqui heard Anna stand up, and footsteps clacking away from the cottage. She opened the door tentatively. Now that Anna had gone, maybe she and Philippe could hit Seventh Circle. But when Jacqui stepped outside again, there was no sign of the French boy anywhere. There were only the remnants of a stubbed-out joint and some torn rolling papers on the curb.

Jacqui felt deflated. She could still go to the club, but somehow, the prospect wasn't as fun or exciting as it had been when she had assumed Philippe would be with her. Besides, now that she thought about it—she *was* tired. Running after three kids all day could do that to a girl. She trudged up the stairs, thinking that her SAT book could keep her company. Somehow, knowing she was doing the right thing wasn't as much consolation as she'd thought.

there's nothing like a maybach to warm a girl's heart

MARA WAS MYSTIFIED TO FIND A FULL CAMERA CREW IN the foyer, setting up overhead lights and screens. One of the guys wearing a headset and carrying a boom almost crashed into Anna's collection of miniature crystal Lladro animal sculptures displayed on a lower shelf. Sugar Perry, wearing a shrunken pink velour hoodie that exposed her midriff, and matching pink velour hot pants, was talking animatedly into the camera. The director, a young guy in faded cords, was kneeling, checking Sugar's image on the monitor, when he noticed Mara hovering by the doorway. "Who's your friend?" he asked, motioning the cameraman to take shots of Mara.

"Oh, that's nobody," Sugar replied in a very bored voice. "She just works here."

But the director ignored Sugar and stared at Mara. "Hi, I'm Randy Braverman from E! Entertainment Network," he said, shaking her hand. "Did Laurie tell you about our show?"

Then Mara remembered. Sugar was starring in a reality show

about rich kids in the Hamptons this summer. The show's premise was to capture the pampered class's day-to-day life, which meant following Sugar everywhere. Laurie had warned them that by working for the Perrys, their participation was mandatory. They'd all had to sign release forms earlier in the week.

"What's Garrett's car doing here?" Sugar asked, looking out the bay window, where a sleek Mercedes Maybach had pulled up to the driveway.

"That's my ride," Mara explained, inching toward the door and hoping to get out of there as quickly as possible.

"*You're* going out with Garrett Reynolds?" Sugar asked, unable to keep the shock from her voice.

"Who's going out with Garrett Reynolds?" Poppy Perry demanded, walking down the stairs. Poppy was a little miffed she hadn't been chosen for the show. Earlier that year their publicist had released a memo to the press requesting that the Perry twins not be called "the Perry twins" in public anymore, but instead be known as "Sugar Perry" and "Poppy Perry" from now on—since they insisted they were two different girls with two different careers. But it had bit Poppy in the ass—apparently, she wasn't as famous as her taller, sexier, more toxic twin.

"I am," Mara said quietly. The Perry twins said Garrett's name in the same way that someone else would say "Prince William" or "Leonardo di Caprio," like he was some kind of god.

Poppy's eyes were like saucers. "No way."

"Funny, he didn't mention anything about it last night," Sugar said, looking at Mara as if Mara had done something wrong.

"What's it like, dating one of the richest guys in the Hamptons?" Randy Braverman asked, the boom suddenly over Mara's head and the cameras directed on her.

"We're not dating. I mean, it's our first—I mean, I don't know. He's really nice," Mara stammered. "Sorry. I really need to go," she said, scissoring through the crowd to the front door.

Garrett emerged from the backseat of the car, carrying one long-stemmed white rose for Mara. He had slicked his dark hair back from his forehead, and he looked handsome in a buttercream-colored linen suit.

"Your chariot, milady," Garrett said. "What's going on over here?" he asked, waving to the crowd, who were huddled in the foyer, watching them. The camera was still focused on the two of them, and Sugar was looking dangerously impatient.

Mara accepted the rose and slid inside. "Sugar's taping something for E! You know, the socialite show."

"Ah yes." Garrett grinned. "*Rich and Stupid in the Hamptons.*"

Mara blinked. She'd thought Sugar and Poppy were Garrett's friends—that was the impression she'd gotten from the twins just now—but here he was making fun of them. Maybe he was smarter than he let on.

"Champagne?" he asked, taking a bottle from a cleverly concealed refrigeration unit in the armrest. The Maybach was a cocoon of luxury, with two plasma television screens, wireless headsets, and bucket seats outfitted with full-body massagers.

"They recline all the way down," Garrett smiled naughtily. "But maybe we'll save that for later."

Mara pretended not to hear. She was beginning to worry she'd made a mistake in saying yes to the date, when all she'd wanted to do was find a way to make Ryan see that they were meant to be together. She didn't want to lead Garrett on, especially since he was going to all this trouble.

"You are absolutely gorgeous," Garrett said, reaching over to squeeze her hand. He looked at her admiringly, complimenting her on her dress, her hair, her smile, her perfume, her legs, her shoes. It was nice to feel appreciated, especially since in Sturbridge, she always felt average, and yesterday, in front of Allison and Ryan, she'd felt practically invisible.

The restaurant was a hushed, formal establishment with tuxedoed waiters and silver candelabras. Mara felt clumsy and out of place, even though she didn't look it. As the haughty maitre d' led them to their table, Garrett whispered, "I bet he's wearing women's underwear." Mara stifled a guffaw and stopped feeling intimidated, even if they were by far the youngest people there.

At dinner, Garrett ordered for her, which would have annoyed her if the dishes he'd chosen hadn't been perfectly delicious. Mara never had "torchons of foie gras" or "gently poached langoustines smothered in caviar" before. The most exotic restaurant in Sturbridge was the Baja Fresh. This was by far the best and most interesting meal she'd ever had. Between the fish course and the meat course, the waiter brought out a martini glass filled with cold cucumber sorbet. "A palate cleanser," Garrett explained. Mara gulped it down, relishing the juicy tartness.

She had to admit she was having fun. For sure, Garrett was a tiny bit self-centered—Mara got a little tired of hearing about his opinion on everything from the electoral process, to stem-cell research, to the new Wes Anderson film, to his idea for a great movie (a remake of *Casablanca* in space!)—but since he was so passionate about it, she didn't hold it against him. Aside from his suggestive asides, he was a riot. He had a childish enthusiasm and irreverence that was catching, and against her better instincts, Mara found herself warming to him.

"I'm never eating again," she declared, after putting away a luscious dessert and patting her full stomach. "That was amazing."

Garrett poured the last of the Sauternes into her dessert wine glass. "Cheers," he said. They polished off the bottle of wine—he'd palmed a hundred-dollar bill so the sommelier wouldn't check IDs, and Mara was definitely feeling tipsy. She staggered out of her chair, and Garrett offered her his arm. He steered her gently back to the sedan.

"Where to?" the chauffeur asked, tipping his cap.

Mara shrugged, smiling impishly at Garrett. He really was hot. She could understand why Poppy and Sugar were jealous. Sugar's boyfriend Charlie was attractive, but Eliza said it was thanks to major plastic surgery, and Poppy had recently been dumped by her on-again, off-again boyfriend Leo, who was slightly cross-eyed.

"Seventh Circle?" Garrett suggested.

Mara nodded. Dinner had been so pleasant. It seemed rude to cut the evening short, especially since Garrett was being conscientious.

"My friend works there," she said, smiling as the Maybach accelerated into the night.

celebrities are like two-year-olds: demanding and prone to tantrums

ELIZA HAD FOLLOWED KARTIK AND ALAN'S INSTRUCTIONS to the letter and was dressed in a silver-sequined Sass & Bide minidress that brushed the tops of her thighs—Jessica Simpson owned the only other one that had ever been made—and a pair of four-inch metallic Pierre Hardy heels.

The club glittered under the strobe lights, and the double-height glass liquor cabinet that ran the length of the club along the back wall was an architectural marvel. The bartenders were hooked to mountain-climbing lines, and when a customer ordered a certain drink, they scaled the shelves like trapeze artists and deftly retrieved the requested bottle. It was an entertaining diversion and a cool gimmick. Already, customers were angling for the most-out-of-reach liquor choices, just to look up the sexy bartenders' skirts. Eliza still couldn't believe the transformation from construction site to hot club that had happened practically overnight. She had to hand it to those guys—they knew what they were doing.

But she hadn't figured that working at a nightclub would be quite so demanding. She'd barely had time to hang out with Mara or even ask her what she was doing with Garrett Reynolds, since it had been total chaos at the velvet rope when they'd arrived. Eliza had put them at the best table in the house; Mara was her best friend, and Garrett was a big deal because of his name alone, so it made sense. She only wished that, like them, she could sit down. Between making sure the celebrities were entertained and indulged, keeping the no-names at bay, feeding the press juicy tidbits, and ducking the airborne bartenders scaling the liquor cabinet, Eliza was exhausted. Her nerves were frazzled, and if one more bodyguard demanded that another photographer be tossed out of the club, she would scream.

Already, she was agitated because Ondine Sylvester, a sitcom star who had once dated pop singer Chauncey Raven's husband, was reportedly on her way. This was bad news, because Chauncey and her hubby, Daryl Wolf, a failed backup singer, were front and center in the VIP room. Chauncey's handler demanded that they not let Ondine inside, lest her client become upset. Ondine had two children by Daryl and had been pregnant with a third when Chauncey had come on the scene. Eliza patiently explained to Chauncey's pompous publicist that they couldn't deny Ondine entrance but that she could promise to seat Ondine on the opposite side of the room. It was important to keep Chauncey happy, since she was the bigger celebrity at the club, but Eliza also understood that they couldn't afford to alienate Ondine either, since they needed as many famous people in the house as possible.

"Eliza—someone at the front for you—says he knows you," Eliza's headset crackled.

"Got it. On my way," she replied, straightening her headset. God, it was probably some old friend from high school trying to get inside, Eliza thought. She'd already let Taylor and Lindsay in, just to show that there were no hard feelings from last summer. Plus, how much fun was it to be the one who held their evening in her hands?

She walked to the front door and saw Jeremy—all six-four of him, looking a bit rumpled in a gray pinstriped suit and a loosened necktie. She'd forgotten how gorgeous he was. His chestnut hair was combed back high from his forehead and curled underneath his ears. He'd told her he would stop by the club that night, but a part of her hadn't believed that he would actually show up. He looked so handsome and businesslike in his suit, and the sight of his red tie askew made her love him even more.

"I told them you asked me to meet you here, but they wouldn't let me in." He grinned.

"It's good, Rudolph," Eliza said to the burly bouncer, smiling at Jeremy.

"Lotsa people say they know Eliza tonight," Rudolph said menacingly to Jeremy, even as he unhooked the velvet rope.

"Rudolph—I'm taking a five-minute break. If Ondine arrives, beep me on the headset."

Eliza led Jeremy by the hand to the back garden, where patrons who'd had enough of the pounding techno beat and relentless posing went for a smoke.

"What's with the suit?" she asked playfully. She didn't want to appear overly excited to see him, even though she was bursting with happiness.

"I'm interning at Morgan Stanley. I-banking," he said.

"Wow. That's awesome!" she said, impressed. Only last summer, Eliza had hated twentysomething investment banker types who rented share-houses in the Hamptons and thought they were entitled to everything. But looking at Jeremy in his suit, I-banking suddenly seemed a lot sexier.

"Yeah, it is. They work me like a dog, though. I'm there until three, four A.M. every night. I didn't think I could get away this weekend, but thankfully we closed on the RFP," he said, talking in financial jargon.

Eliza smiled admiringly at him. This was so not the Jeremy from last summer, who had worked as a gardener on the Perry estate. Last year all Jeremy had cared about were dwarf Japanese elm trees and American Beauty roses.

"Where are you staying?" she asked.

"My parents' place, but I'm in the city all week, staying at an apartment the firm rents for us."

"So," Eliza said, taking Jeremy's hand.

"So," replied Jeremy, rubbing his thumb over her Sheer-Bliss-manicured nails.

They stared at each other, feeling suddenly shy to be so near one other again. Eliza hadn't realized she was inching toward him, until she was standing so close that she could feel his breath on her cheek and they were hugging. She had never experienced anything like this before. She and Jeremy belonged together. Even though the year apart had been hard—she'd tried not to ask if he was dating anyone in the many e-mails she sent him, and he'd never mentioned any other girls in the e-mails he sent her—it was just like the first time they'd met, when they couldn't keep their hands off each other.

Before Eliza knew it, he was kissing her, and it was just as sweet as she remembered. "It's been too long," he murmured into her hair. "I thought about you all the time."

"Me too," she said, liking how her head fit snugly under his chin. "My parents are in Westhampton this summer. We got a house," she said, a little proudly. "Do you maybe want to have dinner with us next week?" Eliza wouldn't have invited Jeremy to meet her parents in the past, fearing they would suss out his working-class background immediately and their disapproval would come between her and Jeremy. But looking at him in his suit and hearing him talk about his internship, she couldn't imagine how her parents wouldn't approve of him.

"If I can get out of work. We have a big presentation next week. But I'll try."

Her headset buzzed. "Eliza! Ondine just walked into the VIP room! There are no tables! And she's about to spot Chauncey and Daryl!"

"I've got to go," she said reluctantly pulling away from his embrace.

"Right. I'm beat anyway. It's been a long week."

"I'll call you," she said, fading back inside the club.

"Not if I call you first." He smiled.

Eliza ordered a table brought out from the back kitchen and set up in the far corner of the VIP room for Ondine, so that the happy newlyweds could drink their free cocktails in peace.

jacqui catches a wave, but the boy slips through her fingers

"LEAVE HER," PHILIPPE ADVISED, AS JACQUI TRIED UNSUC-cessfully to rouse Mara from the bed. They had to be in Montauk for the kids' first surfing lesson by nine, and they wouldn't be able to make it if they waited for Little Miss Hangover to wake up.

Jacqui gave Mara one last shake and was rewarded with a bleary groan. "Mffpphhh," Mara said, turning to her side and burying her head under the pillows.

Mara had stumbled in near dawn, laughing hysterically when she'd climbed into the nearest bed and landed on Philippe. Jacqui and Philippe had helped her into the bottom bunk, Jacqui taking care to cover her friend with a blanket before unzipping her out of her dress. They had tucked her in like one of the kids, and the next morning they looked down at her like bemused parents.

"She's a partier, huh?" Philippe asked a few minutes later, as he and Jacqui collected the kids and all their aquatic equipment, piling the latter into the back of the Range Rover.

"Not usually," Jacqui said, defending her friend as she strapped Cody into his car seat and grabbed Zoë's doll out of William's hands and returned it to the whimpering little girl.

Jacqui was a little annoyed with Philippe. She was bummed to have missed Eliza's opening night at the club. She still had no idea where he'd spent the rest of the evening last night. It wasn't any of her business, but she was a little irritated that he'd paid more attention to Anna than he had to her. Rules were rules, and she didn't plan on breaking hers, but Jacqui wasn't accustomed to playing second banana to anyone.

Philippe backed the SUV out of the driveway, and they were to the private road when Dr. Abraham, in a red bathrobe and flippers, came running out of the house, flagging them down. The kids grumbled as the doctor hauled himself into the car.

"Thank you," the doctor nodded, huffing and puffing and buckling his seat belt.

"Ah, the good doctor," Philippe said cheerfully. "You need to monitor the children's physical activities, yes?" he asked, discreetly motioning toward a large tote bag filled with sunscreen and books. "The beach behavior?"

"Indeed, indeed," Dr. Abraham replied.

When they arrived in Montauk, the two surfing instructors, Bree, a squat, toothy girl with blond dreadlocks, and Roy, a laid-back Hawaiian guy who kept giving them hang-ten hand signals, showed them where to change. Anna had bought all the kids matching black full-body wet suits and the most high-tech equipment, including battery-powered homing devices on their ankle chains that attached to their fiberglass surfboards. Bree handed Jacqui and Philippe wet suits as well, explaining that the cute little string bikini Jacqui was wearing would get totally torn off her body by the waves, eliciting looks of excitement and then disappointment from all the males present.

Once everyone had changed, they paddled out on their boards in the ocean. The smaller waves swelled close to shore, so they didn't have to go too far. Bree and Roy took the two youngest between them, advising William to follow.

"Ouch!" William said, as a wave crested and he smacked himself on the face with his board.

"Hold it out like this," Philippe said, holding his borrowed board at arm's length and grasping the rails.

A large wave lifted all of them up a few feet, drawing frightened screams from Cody, who was wearing water wings with his wet suit.

"Boards at the sides, facing the beach!" Roy directed, cupping his hands over his mouth. "Keep an eye on the waves and choose one that looks like it can hold you, like this," he said. "Then pull yourself up on the board. Paddle out, let the wave take you."

"Easier said than done," Jacqui noted, pulling herself up on the board only to fall back on the other side. "*Merda!*"

"Look at me! Look at me!" Zoë said, slipping out of Bree's reach and paddling furiously as a wave brought her to shore.

"Nice one, *mahalo*!" Roy said, giving another hang-ten signal.

"Cowabunga!" William yelled, diving straight into the sand as a wave tossed him backward. "I'm okay! I'm okay!" he said, resurfacing and spitting out ocean water.

Philippe ducked into a wave, paddling furiously, then emerged, standing straight up on his board, cruising to the sand. He ran back to the water, laughing. "I haven't done that in years." His whole face was lit up, and his eyes were gleaming.

"Wow! *Surpreendente!*" Jacqui said. "I didn't know you could surf."

"Only a little. It's not that hard," he said, coaching her. "There, get that one. . . . Pull up, pull up, *bien*! Ah, fantastic! Go, go, go!" he cheered, as Jacqui coasted gracefully down to the beach.

They watched the kids bob up and down for a while, satisfied that Roy and Bree were taking good care of their charges, then retreated back to shore, where Dr. Abraham was snoozing underneath his umbrella.

"Looks like they're paying him to take a vacation," Jacqui noted dryly.

Philippe nodded. "Good thing we're working so hard," he teased as he spread out their towels. "The only thing I hate is when it sloshes around," he said, jumping up and down.

Jacqui nodded and unzipped her suit, peeling it from her body. She could feel Philippe staring at her, even though she wasn't looking at him.

"You are very beautiful," he stated, in the same way that someone would say, "The sun is hot" or "The earth is round," like it was simply a fact of life and nothing to get all hot and bothered about.

"Thank you," she said, meeting his gaze with her level one.

"You must get told that a lot, I'm sure. It must get extremely . . . *ennuyeux* . . . uh, boring," Philippe said.

"It is, actually," Jacqui said seriously.

"Then maybe I should just say you are very ugly," he teased.

Jacqui threw a snorkel at him. He was cute, but he was also quick and she liked that. She hugged her legs to her chest and reluctantly cracked open her SAT book. Her first class was tomorrow night, and as much as she just wanted to spend the day flirting with Philippe, she couldn't afford to be distracted.

Philippe's cell rang again, which it seemed to do constantly. Jacqui wondered how someone who'd never been to the Hamptons could have made so many friends so quickly.

"'Allo?" he asked, snapping open his phone. He spoke in rapid French, then excused himself, hoisting his backpack on his shoulder.

"Where are you going?" Jacqui called.

Philippe held up his finger to say, "Just a minute," but he kept walking away toward the boardwalk. Jacqui noticed several girls watching him from behind their oversized Gucci and Chanel frames, as well as a few guys checking him out from under their striped umbrellas. Philippe was giving everyone, male and female, the same flirtatious smile. Jacqui sighed and dropped her head to look at her book. She would never understand the French.

that's why it's called page six six six

LATER THAT SAME MORNING, MARA WOKE UP TO FIND herself alone in the au pairs' room. It was almost eleven-thirty, and Philippe and Jacqui were nowhere to be found. Mara was surprised she'd slept so late and that neither of them had woken her up. Last night was a hazy blur. She remembered dancing wildly when the old rock song "Livin' on a Prayer" came on, crashing into Eliza, and trading shopping stories with Chauncey Raven, the beleaguered pop star who'd recently had her second quickie marriage in Vegas, who was sitting at the next table. She'd also spent a good part of the evening perched on Garrett's lap, since a bunch of his friends had shown up and they'd had to squeeze into the banquette, but she'd fended off his good-night kiss when he'd dropped her off at four in the morning.

Mara shuffled into the main house, which was reverberating with the sound of the Reynolds Castle's jackhammers. She shook her head—all that pounding was not what she needed right now—and walked into the kitchen, where antique French cabinetry covered every surface, even the Sub-Zero fridge. She realized that maybe the Reynolds Castle was just like every house in the Hamptons, just bigger and more obvious. The kitchen was empty save for Madison, who was weighing a boiled chicken breast on a kitchen scale. Mara watched as the girl carefully cut it in half, weighed it again, and then put it on a plate with several raw baby carrots.

"What are you doing?"

Madison glared. "Nothing."

Mara pulled up a stool next to her and began to assemble breakfast, slicing a banana and pouring two-percent milk over a bowl of cereal. "You know, Madison, when I was younger, I was kind of chubby. But when I turned fourteen, my metabolism kicked in when I was playing a lot of soccer, and I lost a lot of weight."

"I hate soccer," Madison sulked, slamming the door behind her.

Mara sighed. She picked up a copy of the *New York Post*, which had been opened to the Page Six column. *HAS THE REYNOLDS HEIR FOUND LOVE?* screamed the headline, above a picture of Mara perched on Garrett's lap from the night before.

She was leaning on Garrett's arm, laughing at what he was saying. Garrett was smirking into the camera, holding a fizzing bottle of champagne in one hand, with the other clasped firmly around

Mara's waist. Aside from a few snide mentions about the hundred-thousand-square-foot "Frankenstein Castle" the Reynoldses were building in East Hampton, the accompanying article was nearly identical to one about her and Ryan from the summer before, detailing how the sexy young couple had been caught canoodling at the hottest club of the season. *Canoodling?* She'd only been sitting on his lap! Okay, so maybe he'd nuzzled her neck a little. . . .

A pit formed in her stomach. She wondered if Ryan had been the one to leave the paper on the table. She picked up and sniffed a half-empty cup sitting next to the paper. Green tea. Ryan was only one in the Perry household who drank green tea.

Just then, Sugar walked in, panther-skinny and sweaty from a morning yoga session. The same two-man camera crew from last night followed her.

"Oh, hi," Sugar said. "Is that Page Six?" She walked over to read over Mara's shoulder. Sugar looked up from the picture and regarded Mara thoughtfully. "You guys should hang out with me and Charlie some time."

One of the Perry twins being nice to her? Mara couldn't believe it. Last summer Sugar hadn't even been able to remember her name. She'd called her Marta or Maria or Mary.

"We're having a party on his yacht next weekend. Close friends only. Bring Gar. It'll rock."

"Yeah, maybe," Mara mumbled as Sugar shrugged and smiled into the cameras, tossing her hair back and puffing out her chest.

"C'mon, guys," Sugar told the crew. "Meet me in the outdoor shower."

Mara stared at Page Six, wondering if there was any way Ryan would want to talk to her after seeing that picture. That was the thing about pictures—they were worth a thousand words, but sometimes they weren't the right ones.

nothing spells love like a
car full of goody bags

AT END OF THE FOLLOWING WEEK, MARA MADE HER
way to the screening room for the first weekly progress meeting.
Jacqui and Philippe were supposed to join her as soon as they
returned from taking the boys to some kind of boot camp for the
day. The two of them were obviously getting friendly and liked to
do chores together if they could.

Mara planned to complain about Dr. Abraham at the meeting. He'd lectured her when she'd given Cody a hug after he'd
stubbed his toe, telling her direly, "Positive reinforcement after a
painful experience is unlikely to build character," and then asked
her if she knew how he could get a VIP table at Seventh Circle a
few minutes later. There was something off about the guy.

After sitting in the dark for fifteen minutes, it became clear
to Mara that neither Anna nor Kevin would materialize. No surprise there. The meetings were something Anna had insisted
upon last summer as well, even though neither she nor Kevin
ever attended. Mara shrugged and walked out of the room.

Madison and Zoë were waiting for her to take them to yoga.

They walked out the front door to see a large delivery truck parked in the Perrys' driveway. Several uniformed workers were unloading racks of clothing as well as dozens of black shopping bags with pink tissue paper sticking out of the top. An overly tanned, clothes-hanger-skinny woman in a white tank top that read YOUR BOYFRIEND WANTS ME and low-riding blue jeans was directing the action.

"What's going on?" Mara asked Laurie, who was surveying the spectacle with a caustic eye.

"I'm not sure, but I think it's for you," Laurie said.

"Hi! Mara Waters? Mitzi Goober!" the woman in the white tank top said, saying her last name with a Frenchified lilt, so it sounded like "*Giubaire*" rather than the name of a popular candy. She thrust a muscular and bony arm in Mara's direction. "Wow! I would never have recognized you. You are *so* much prettier than your pictures!"

"Thanks, I think . . ." Mara said, her forehead descending.

She'd thought things would die down after the photo of her and Garrett was published in the *Post*, but the following week it had popped up in *Hamptons*, *Hamptons Life*, *Hamptons Living*, *Hamptons Country*, and *Hamptons Luxury* magazines. She never had a chance to explain the photo to Ryan, since whenever they ran into each other—just that morning they'd bumped into each other in the pool—he basically ignored her. It was heartbreaking how aloof he was, but it did help that Garrett was being so persistent about a second date. He'd already sent her so many flow-ers, the au pairs' room looked like a funeral parlor.

A shot of Mara alone, in the lavender Zac Posen dress, had ultimately ended up on the party page of *Vogue*, under the head-ing *Lilac Ladies*, between a photo of Jennifer Connelly in a bow-tied lavender Chloé dress and one of Aerin Lauder in a purple Valentino shift. Mara had been back in the Hamptons for two weeks, but already she was eliciting stares of barely concealed jeal-ousy, or just plain curiosity, everywhere she went. She felt like a freak and a fraud: There she was, in the pages of a glossy maga-zine posing in Jacqui's designer dress, while in reality, she was schlepping the kids to the dentist, wiping Cody's bottom, and trying to coerce Madison into eating something more than clear chicken broth and nonfat string cheese.

"Anyway, dollink, as I was just explaining to your assistant here . . ." Mitzi was saying.

Doll rink? Mara was confused. *Doll tint?* What the hell was Mitzi saying? *Dog fink?* It was hard to follow her rat-a-tat delivery.

"I'm Anna Perry's assistant," Laurie cut in.

"Sure. Whatever," Mitzi said as she motioned the delivery men to grab the rest of the bags from the truck.

"Mara is an au pair," Laurie said indignantly.

"An au pair! How cute! Groovy!" Mitzi said. "Listen, Mara, I've got a hot new designer who wants to dress you—several, in fact—and these are all gifts for you to wear around town."

"For me?" Mara said, watching the guys set down bag after bag on the grass next to the driveway.

"Sure, sure, sure! Just make sure to mention their names when people ask you what you're wearing. Shoshanna sent her whole summer collection. She loved the photos of you in her dress last year, and she thinks you might like a few pieces. Okay to just leave them here?"

"This is really nice, Mitzi, but uh, I don't know."

"Wait! Wait! Best part. Almost forgot." Mitzi grabbed a black velvet case from her oversized Birkin bag. "A gift. Open."

Mara opened the case. Inside was a strand of luminescent pearls nestled on a velvet pillow.

"Mikimotos. They're only the cultured ones, sorry. But if you could remember to mention them if you can . . ." Mitzi smiled.

"I don't know if I can accept these," Mara said nervously.

"What are you talking about? Please! You deserve it! You're so fabulous! God, why can't I get my hair to do that?" Mitzi said, sticking out her tongue and pulling at her hair. Mara had never met anyone as full of energy and enthusiasm as Mitzi Goober. She was like your new best friend, cheerleader, and guru all in one. She was giving Mara a headache.

As the messengers began to unload a second rolling rack, Mara tried to get them to put it back on the truck, with Madison and Zoë, wide-eyed at all the loot, at her heels. "Mitzi! Wait! Really, I can't!"

"Nonsense! Do you know how hard it is to find someone who

fits into a sample size? Please. It would be such a great favor to my designers. They are your biggest fans."

Fans? She was an au pair who'd posed for a few pictures, and now she had a following?

Mitzi rattled a key chain in front of Mara's nose. "What are you driving? That Range Rover over there? It's so bulky, don't you think?"

"It's the Perrys', actually."

"I'd really love it if you could test-drive this new BMW convertible," Mitzi said, thrusting the keys into Mara's hands and motioning to a shiny black car on the driveway.

"A car?" Mara said, her mouth hanging open.

"For the whole summer. Every day we'll get someone to fill the gas tank and put some treats in there for you. Fun-fun-fun! So you won't have to worry."

Mara stared at the BMW keys. This was crazy. And exciting. She could actually *keep* all this stuff?

Zoë and Madison had begun rifling through the racks. "Oooh, look at this!" Madison said, holding up a black jersey Gucci halter top. "Pretty!" Zoë said as she wrapped herself in a lacy shawl.

"Wait! Mitzi!" Mara said, running to catch up with the publicist, who had hopped into a vintage Citroën and was pulling out of the driveway. "I just—I don't know if this is right," Mara said, leaning in the window.

Mitzi put a hand to Mara's mouth, smushing her lipstick. "Dollink!"

Doe wink? Door blink? Mara wondered.

"Don't be boring! Just remember, mention my clients when you talk to the press. Deal? Have a great summer! And I hope you come to my party at Seventh Circle next week! Toodles!"

Mitzi pulled out of the driveway and the Toyota Prius pulled in.

"Who was that?" Jacqui asked, getting out of the car with Philippe and the boys.

Mara looked around at what Mitzi had left her—two rolling racks full of designer clothes, several bags of shoes and accessories, a velvet case of pearls, and a shiny black BMW convertible.

"Um, I'm not really sure," Mara said, amazed at her good fortune. "My fairy godmother?"

guess who's coming to dinner?

TWO WEEKS AFTER ELIZA AND JEREMY WERE REUNITED at Seventh Circle, Eliza opened the door to find him standing on her doorstep with a bouquet of flowers. They had seen each other only once since then—Jeremy's brutal work schedule kept him in the city more often than not, and they'd already had to reschedule dinner twice. Her parents were totally harassing her to let them meet her "young man." They were old-fashioned that way, and Eliza hoped that the dinner would go well, or at least go quickly, so she and Jeremy could get out of there and finally be alone.

"For your mom," Jeremy said, handing her the white Astor lilies. Their clean fragrance filled the room.

"That's so sweet. Come on in," Eliza said. She'd worn her hair back in a demure chignon and had tied a black satin ribbon with an antique locket around her neck. She knew Jeremy liked it when she looked pretty and girlish, and so she'd chosen her clothes carefully—a white Chloé eyelet cotton dress and pink Delman ballet flats. She was pleased that he looked so professional in his tan linen suit and sky blue dress shirt. He'd loosened his conservatively striped tie just a bit, and he looked the perfect picture of a young, successful banker.

"Dad, this is Jeremy. Jeremy, this is my dad, Ryder Thompson," Eliza said, leading Jeremy into the living room. Her father, a tall, large man with a gleaming crown of silver hair, stood up to shake Jeremy's hand.

Ryder had worked on Wall Street, too, before he'd been caught dipping a little too often into the bank's coffers. Eliza still couldn't believe it had been such a big deal: It was his company, wasn't it? Didn't that count for something? Sure, she remembered how they used the company jet for weekend trips to Paris, but so what? The papers had said that even Eliza's two-hundred-thousand-dollar Sweet Sixteen party at the Rainbow Room was paid for by the company's dime, but plenty of her dad's associates were there, so it *was* sort of like a business function. In any case, that hadn't stopped the subsequent investigation, lawsuit, and humiliation. The Thompson family had weathered it as best they could, keeping their chins up and finally hightailing it to Buffalo when Manhattan became unbearable and unaffordable.

Her parents had made it clear that it was very important that Eliza date a suitable boy, someone appropriate to her background and breeding, despite everything that had happened in the last couple of years. Eliza hoped Jeremy would pass her parents' litmus test. They could be a little strict when they chose to be, and for the first time Eliza missed the freedom she'd experienced last summer, when she'd lived on her own and hadn't had to answer to anyone except the Perrys, who were away or indifferent most of the time.

"Gin?" Ryder asked Jeremy, holding up a silver cocktail shaker.

"Whatever Eliza is drinking is fine, thanks, Mr. Thompson," Jeremy replied.

Eliza's dad frowned as he poured Jeremy a glass of white wine but made no comment. The four of them sank into the linen couch.

"I must apologize—this is not to our standard," Eliza's mother, Billie, said, her hands nervously fluttering about her throat as she looked at the collection of porcelain dolls in a china cabinet with distaste. "But Eliza did so want to be back in the Hamptons this year, and we thought . . ."

"It's very nice," Jeremy assured her. "I like these old houses. They have a feeling of security to them, don't you think?"

Eliza's mother smiled warmly at him. "I like older architecture as well."

"Jeremy grew up in the Hamptons," Eliza offered, unwittingly trying to make it sound like Jeremy was more like them. Not that she really cared what her parents thought—she didn't think like they did anymore, not really, anyway. If she did, she would have been after Garrett Reynolds, not Jeremy Stone. But it would just be so much easier if they liked him.

"Oh, where?" Billie asked, brightening.

"Southampton," Jeremy said.

There was a murmur of approval from the Thompsons. "Do you know the Rosses? Courtney started that lovely school. We almost moved out here too, so that Eliza could go there."

"I know Mrs. Ross," Jeremy allowed. He didn't add that he was their gardener, to Eliza's relief.

"Where in Southampton?" Eliza's father inquired.

Jeremy told him.

"Ah, is that in the township?" Ryder asked, referring to the considerably more modest section of single-family homes in Southampton called the township.

Jeremy nodded.

"How quaint," Billie nodded with a strained smile.

"What does your father do?" Ryder inquired.

"Jeremy's dad runs his own business." Eliza interjected. She could see where this was going.

"What kind of enterprise?" her dad asked.

"He owns a fish and bait shop on Route 27," Jeremy replied, before Eliza could fudge some other euphemism like, "He's in the shipping industry."

"Is it the one with the big neon salmon on the door?" Billie asked.

"That's it!" Jeremy slapped his thigh.

"I think Colombia got some lovely oysters from there the other day, darling," Billie said, nodding to her husband. "They were delicious. So fresh."

Jeremy beamed, but Eliza felt the burden of impending disaster. This was not going well. Eliza knew her parents were snobs' snobs. They could figure out somebody's place in the social hierarchy in a heartbeat, and Eliza could see they were writing Jeremy off.

"Where do you go to college, dear?" Billie asked, continuing the interrogation as they sat down for dinner.

"I go to State," Jeremy said, wiping his mouth with a linen napkin. "SUNY."

Ryder Thompson turned to his wife. "Isn't that Woody Allen's wife?" he joked.

Eliza stepped in. This was too painful. "He means State University of New York, Dad. In Nassau. It's not far from here."

"New York has a wonderful state university system," Billie said graciously.

Eliza squirmed in her seat. Jeremy was the first person in his family ever to go to college, and he was really proud of that. *Don't hate me,* her eyes pleaded, wanting him to look up so he could see how much she was on his side, but Jeremy kept his head down for the rest of the evening.

After coffee, the Thompsons took their leave, wishing

Jeremy a courteous good night and reminding Eliza about her curfew.

"So do you want to go for a ride somewhere? Maybe take a walk on the beach?" Eliza asked, standing up from the table. She wanted to apologize for her parents, but she was still holding on to the hope that Jeremy hadn't noticed they were total snobs.

"Nah," Jeremy shook his head. "I have an early meeting tomorrow. I should get back."

Eliza's face fell. They weren't even going to hang out? It was her one night off from the club and she'd been looking forward to seeing him all week.

Jeremy slung his coat jacket over his shoulder and walked toward the door. Eliza opened it for him and followed him to the porch.

"What about dinner next week at Lunch—just the two of us?" Eliza asked. She hated how desperate she sounded.

"Maybe." He sighed. "Things are really busy at the office."

"Don't go," she said, her lips trembling. She lifted up her chin to be kissed, willing him to understand.

Jeremy sighed and looked like he was about to walk away, but he bent his head down instead. They stood under the porch light kissing for what seemed to Eliza to be a sweet eternity.

"I love you, you know," she said, muffled into his shirt.

"I know," he said, reluctantly pulling away. "But I've got to get back into work early tomorrow, and I can't miss the last train." He climbed into his rusty pickup truck, the one remnant of his former occupation.

Eliza watched him drive away and wondered when she would see him again. She hadn't failed to notice that when she'd said, "I love you," he hadn't said it back.

kryptonite is to superman as boys are to jacqui

TO JACQUI'S CHAGRIN, THE SAT PREP CLASS SHE'D SIGNED up for was filled with overachieving rich kids who were striving for nothing less than a perfect showing—which made her scores on the first diagnostic test even more depressing. Jacqui had just stuffed her SAT books in the backseat of the Prius that evening when she saw Philippe ride up on a Vespa. He took off his helmet and shook out his hair. "*Arrête!*" he said when he saw Jacqui.

She leaned against the door of the car and smiled. "What's up?"

He shrugged, smiling his devastating grin. "*Pas beaucoup.* Where are you going?"

"Class," she explained. "It's Wednesday, remember?"

Jacqui had told him about the class the other night, when he'd stumbled in around midnight and found her studying her SAT book. She told him about her SAT prep course, and he'd affectionately teased her about what a distraction she must be to

110

all the dorks in the class. Philippe's plan for his life was to win the Rolex tennis invitational, turn pro, follow the circuit, and generally have a great time bouncing from one sunny resort town to another. His entire ambition in life was to become a tennis bum.

"Come play pool with me instead," Philippe invited. "You can skip one class, no? He smiled roguishly, looking her up and down in an inviting manner.

Jacqui bit her lip. Playing pool with Philippe sounded like so much more fun than sitting in a damp basement solving word problems. She'd hardly had a bit of excitement in weeks. To think that she, Jacqui, was actually the one who was shouldering most of the work with the kids. She was proud of that, since she did have a knack for it, but she missed having fun.

Philippe took her hand, and they tiptoed to the main house. They made their way to the screening room, where a billiard table sat in the corner. One of the most amazing things about the Perrys' house was that there was hardly ever anyone home to enjoy its wealth of amusements. The twins were always out at some party, Ryan kept to his room when he was home, and the many toys—the sixteen-foot projection screen, the ATVs parked next to the beachfront, the vintage PacMan and pinball machines—mostly went unused. Philippe racked the balls and Jacqui broke, sinking a solid yellow ball in a corner pocket.

"So where've you been anyway?" she asked, rubbing chalk

on her pool cue. Philippe had been MIA for a few days. She leaned over the table to assess her next shot. She flubbed an easy one, sending a ball to the opposite corner instead of the near pocket.

"I had to go visit the French consulate and Anna needed me to help with something, so we spent a couple of days in New York," he said, walking around the table and studying the angles for his shot.

"Mmmm . . . Just the two of you?"

Philippe shrugged and sank a striped ball. "*Oui*. Have you been to their townhouse in the city? It's beautiful," he said.

Jacqui felt ridiculous for feeling a little jealous, but she did. She'd been so sure Philippe was interested in her—but even though they slept next to each other almost every night, he never even tried to make a move. Even though she'd promised herself not to be distracted by boys this summer, she hadn't counted on not being a distraction herself.

"I love New York," Jacqui said dreamily. She'd never actually even been to the city, but the place loomed large in her imagination. The busy streets, the people, the little cafes, the nightclubs, the shopping. Jacqui loved Brazil, but she was looking forward to making her future in New York. "It's the best city in the world."

Philippe grunted, leaning down for a shot.

"I want to stay in New York next year," she said wistfully.

He looked up from the pool table. "*Pourquoi?*"

She told him excitedly about her plans for Stuyvesant and hopefully NYU and how she hoped Anna would help get her a nanny position if she did a good job this summer.

They played, matching each other ball for ball, until only the black eight-ball was left. It was in a precarious position, and Jacqui hunkered down, twisting her body so she could aim with the cue.

"You have to keep one leg on the floor," Philippe reminded her, as Jacqui's mule heels dangled from the table.

"I'm trying!" she laughed.

"Like this," Philippe said, coming up behind her and gently guiding her arms. She let him press on the stick and release it. The ball shot into the corner pocket.

"So who won?" Jacqui asked, turning her head toward him. Philippe still had his arms around her.

"Call it even," he said, leaning down to smell her hair. He pressed against her back, and Jacqui felt the heat from his body. It was too much to resist. She melted into him, shuddering as he planted soft kisses down her neck. She closed her eyes and turned toward him. As if he'd read her mind, he gently lowered her to the table, bumping her head on the overhead light.

"Oops!" she laughed, pulling him down on top of her. She felt his hands twine through her hair as he kissed her neck and shoulders. She snaked her hands up behind his back.

"Jacqui?"

The lights in the screening room suddenly blazed on.

Jacqui pushed Philippe off her, unintentionally kicking up the pool stick, which smacked him squarely on the forehead.

"Ouch!"

"What were you guys doing?" Zoë asked, holding a teddy bear. "Why are you on the pool table?"

This was *exactly* why the No More Boys rule had been invented.

nobody puts
mara in the corner

IT WAS ANOTHER BUSY NIGHT AT SEVENTH CIRCLE, AND
Eliza was trying to keep up with the rush of impatient clubgoers
storming the velvet rope. Kartik had advised her to let guests
trickle in slowly, in small groups of two or three. That way there
was always a long line at the door, which made the club look even
more popular than it was.

Eliza scanned the crowd, looking for Jeremy. She hoped he
would stop by the club again, but so far, he hadn't shown up. She
hadn't seen him since the disastrous dinner with her parents the
week before. She'd left him a couple of messages on his cell phone
and at work, where some schmuck had answered the phone and
asked her to spell her name twice. But he'd never called her back.

"Name?" she asked an older woman in a beige pantsuit who
had wrestled her way to the front of the line.

"Margot Whitman," the lady answered sharply.

Eliza ran a nail against the list, searching intently. *Wilson
(Owen), Wilson (Luke plus one), Williams (Venus & Serena),*

W, Women's Wear Daily. "I'm sorry," she concluded. "You're not on the list," she said flatly. Kartik had advised her that the guest list rule only applied to "civilians." Models, or other fearsomely pretty girls, as well as celebrities and other VIPs could always get in, regardless of their guest list status. But as for regular people—which this woman clearly was—they could freeze in hell before they were allowed inside Seventh Circle.

"I'm Alan's mother," the woman declared. "Is this some kind of joke? Can you get my good-for-nothing son out here to let me in? This is ridiculous. I've got clients waiting here."

"I'm sorry, do you want to try Alan on his cell phone to confirm? I can't do anything," Eliza apologized.

The woman threw her arms up. "This is bull! I am his mother! Now let me inside!"

Eliza held her ground. Alan's voice echoed in her brain. *The List is God. It could be my mother out there, but if she's not on the list, tough luck.* What if this woman was some kind of impostor? Although she did have Alan's receding chin and bug eyes. But rules were rules, and for once, Eliza didn't want to break them. It was too much fun to say no sometimes.

"Sorry. I can't help you," Eliza decided. "Please step to the side. You're not on the list. Next!"

"Hey, E," a familiar voice said, and a hand tapped her shoulder.

Eliza's heart leapt for a moment—Jeremy had arrived! But when she looked up, it was Ryan who was standing in front of the velvet rope. He was wearing his linen sweater that brought out the green in his eyes, and a pair of jeans. Totally not dress-code-worthy, but rules didn't apply to guys who were as hand-some as Ryan Perry.

"Oh, Ryan, hey." Eliza smiled, nodding to Rudolph to unhook the rope.

"Crazy night, huh?" Ryan asked, motioning to the teeming, seething mass of people who stared angrily back since he was able to cut the line. Someone even threw a beer bottle, which smashed right in front of Eliza's feet, and Rudolph immediately hustled the frustrated civilian away.

"You have no idea," Eliza said, shaking her head at the mess. "What is it about nightclubs that bring out the worst in people? The regular people insist they're on the guest list, the guest list people demand VIP tables, the VIPs want . . . oh, God, well, they want everything. The other day I had to babysit Naomi Campbell's fur coat. Apparently it needed a massage." Eliza laughed.

Ryan shrugged, grinning. "Ah, you can handle it."

Eliza handed him some free-drink tickets. "I guess." She rolled her eyes. It was nice to see Ryan again. They'd hardly seen each other at all since they'd gotten back, maybe because of what had happened in Palm Beach. Damn Palm Beach. Eliza wished, not for the first time, that she'd never even gone there.

"Eliza! Hey! Over here!"

Eliza turned and saw Mara and Garrett push their way through the crowd. She felt another burst of happiness at seeing a familiar face and waved back, ushering them to the front of the line as well.

Ryan turned around too, but his face clouded as soon as he saw Mara and Garrett. "I should go," he told Eliza, bumping a fist on her shoulder. "I'm meeting Allison inside."

"Where you going, Perry?" Garrett called.

Mara saw Ryan walk away without saying hello, and her heart ached. He looked so cute in that sweater. It was her favorite sweater. Last summer she'd borrowed it from him when they were on the beach and it got cold, and the sweater was so big, it reached down to her knees.

For two weeks, Mara had brushed Garrett off with excuses, saying she had to stay and watch the kids, or she was tired, or that she was busy with something else. But yesterday, she'd finally caved. She'd bumped into Ryan and Allison walking on the beach and then come home to the racks of fabulous clothes. It seemed a shame not to let them see the light of a paparazzi bulb. Wasn't that what she was supposed to do anyway? Wear the clothes and pose for pictures?

"How are you?" Mara gushed, giving Eliza a dramatic double air-kiss. "Where have you been?"

"I've been, um, good," Eliza said, feeling guilty about Palm Beach all over again. "I've been here. You know where to find me."

"All right, but seriously, we need to hang out!" Mara said. "Anyway, do you think we could get a table? My heels are, like, killing me."

Last summer Mara had lived in either Reeboks or flip-flops. Eliza noticed she was wearing a pair of shockingly high Manolo Blahnik sandals with two bands of sparkling rhinestone straps at the toe and ankle. The same ones Eliza had wanted, except they'd been all out of her size. Where had she gotten those?

Eliza led them through the double doors, past the bi-level dance floor, which glittered under the strobe lights. The music was deafening, and the crowd was a mix of underdressed women and overdressed guys. Eliza noticed a particularly amorous couple stretched out on one of the king-sized ottomans and wondered if she should throw a coat over them.

"Garrett, my man," Kartik said, as Eliza seated Mara and Garrett. "Good to see you."

Then he turned to Eliza. "Did you let in those eyesores in the back?" Kartik accused, jerking a thumb toward two nondescript men and their shellacked dates, who were eagerly looking around, taking pictures with their camera phones.

Eliza shook her head. They must have made dinner reservations to get inside.

"Turn the lights down around them, will you? They're seriously killing the mood. And I want them gone before Mitzi gets here."

Eliza nodded. She asked the busboy to dim the lights, then walked back to where she'd sat Mara and Garrett, not realizing she'd put them uncomfortably close to Ryan and Allison's table.

"How about shopping tomorrow?" Mara asked, after they'd

119

given their drink orders to the cocktail waitress, and the bartender promptly zoomed up the wall to retrieve a bottle of the expensive Finnish vodka that Garrett had ordered. "We get paid!"

"Well, I don't, but yeah, sure," Eliza said, a little more tersely than she'd intended.

Mara saw Ryan across the VIP room, leaning against the bar with Allison. The tall Nordic blonde was laughing at something Ryan was saying, and it was killing Mara how Ryan was smiling back at her, his dimples flashing.

"Penny for your thoughts," Garrett said, handing her the mojito she'd ordered. After Eliza had made the tangy Cuban cocktails that first weekend, they had quickly become Mara's favorite drink. The sugarcane and crushed mint leaves reminded her of the last time she was really happy. Since arriving in the Hamptons, things had not exactly turned out as she'd hoped: Ryan was with another girl, Eliza was being weirdly distant, and she felt like a third wheel around Jacqui and Philippe. Even the kids didn't seem to like her as much as they had last summer.

"I was just thinking . . ." she said, watching as Ryan rubbed Allison's shoulders. Ugh. She turned back to Garrett. "Let's dance."

Garrett smiled. "You got it." He stood up and offered her his hand. They snaked their way to the center of the dance floor, where the crowd was gyrating to Nelly's "Hot in Herre." The song was kind of last year, but it was still a club favorite.

Mara began to swing her hips and feel the music throb against her body. She moved to the beat, dancing sexily around Garrett, letting her hands slide up and down his back, and pressing her legs against his. Garrett, unlike most guys his age, who kept their dancing to a one-two shuffle, could actually move—and he ground his pelvis into Mara's hips in a sinuous, sexy rhythm. Mara lost herself to the sensation of the music, the alcohol, and the feel of his breath against her neck. She turned around, and Garrett pulled her toward him, pressing against her back. He licked the back of her neck, and she raked her fingernails up his thighs behind her.

It was quite a performance—one that Ryan wouldn't be able to miss, but that was sort of the point. Mara sneaked a glance in his direction, and was gratified to see that he'd stopped talking to Allison and was watching Mara with a scowl on his face. Mara tossed her hair back and pulled Garrett closer to her.

"God, you're hot," Garrett said, whispering raggedly in her ear. "Where'd you learn to dance like that?"

Mara smiled slyly. She liked Garrett. But more than that, she liked that being with Garrett made Ryan jealous. Maybe that way, Ryan would do something about it.

On the other side of the club, Alan grabbed Eliza's elbow as she ushered Kit and a crew of Eastern European gazelles to his table. "My mom just reamed me out. She said she couldn't get into the club earlier. What's the deal?" Alan demanded of Eliza.

Eliza froze. "Your mom? Margot Whitman? But she wasn't on the list!" she explained in her defense. "And you said—"

Alan's features relaxed. "She wasn't on the list? Well, in that case . . . hold on . . . *Ma!* You didn't RSVP!" he yelled into his wireless receiver. "How many times do I have to tell you, you gotta RSVP?! No, I can't do it for you! I am a very, very busy man! Why don't you ever listen to me? You don't get in if you're not on the list! Twenty-four hours of labor? C'mon, I run a business here!" Walking away, he patted Eliza on the shoulder, mouthing, "Good job."

never trust a
seven-year-old
to keep a secret

ANNA PERRY FINALLY SHOWED UP FOR A WEEKLY PROGRESS meeting the next day. It was the Friday before the Fourth of July weekend, and she was taking the kids to Nantucket to visit their grandparents. Unfortunately for Anna, Kevin's family didn't believe in help, and so the au pairs were granted a holiday break as well.

"Oh, hello, Mara," Anna said, actually standing up to kiss Mara on both cheeks.

Mara responded graciously, oblivious to Jacqui's puzzled look.

Before heading to Seventh Circle last night, Mara and Garrett had bumped into Anna at the Boys & Girls Club annual harbor fireworks benefit, and Anna had noticed Mara chatting with Jessica Seinfeld. A dinner invitation to the Seinfelds' was the Hamptons biggest "get," and Anna had yet to score one.

"How is everyone today?" Anna asked, looking around the table pleasantly.

Philippe smirked and sat with his feet on top of the table, but

Jacqui squirmed in her chair beside him. She was certain they were going to be fired after being caught fooling around in the game room by Zoë. Since then, she had stayed as far away from him as possible, rebuffing all his attempts to pick up where they'd left off. Jacqui was certain Anna was just relishing the moment before swinging the ax.

Anna went through the progress reports, which were more tragic than usual, even for the Perry kids. Dr. Abraham had reported that William was now showing signs of bipolar disorder on top of ADHD and that he and Cody—who was possibly schizophrenic—would have to be constantly monitored. Zoë still couldn't recognize the Cyrillic alphabet (although she *had* memorized a *Marie Claire* article on how to find your G-spot—Zoë thought it was in her elbow), but Anna was strangely ebullient regardless.

"Rome wasn't built in a day, now was it?" she asked, winking at Philippe while dispensing three cash-filled envelopes. "Jacqui darling, can you stay a bit?" she asked, as they filed out of the room.

"Sure," Jacqui nodded, settling back into her seat apprehensively. Mara gave Jacqui a questioning look as she walked out, but Jacqui pretended not to see it. She hadn't told Mara about Philippe, since she was well aware she'd broken her rule and she didn't want to be lectured about it. She felt stupid enough already.

"First of all, Philippe has told me everything," Anna said, once everyone had left and the door was closed.

This is it. I'm fired, Jacqui thought. *Good-bye, East Hampton. Good-bye, New York. Hello, retail and sales, for the rest of my life.*

"And I think it's an excellent idea." Anna nodded crisply, stuffing her papers into her handbag.

"*Desculpe-me* . . . er . . . pardon?"

"You, staying with us in New York for the year." Anna smiled. "That is what you want, isn't it?"

"Excuse me?"

"So you can finish your senior year in the city. That was the plan, wasn't it? To attend Stuyvesant so you can apply to NYU?"

Jacqui nodded, speechless. Philippe had told Anna about that? Why? And why was Anna looking so happy about it?

"I think that can definitely be arranged," Anna nodded thoughtfully. She blew her nose daintily on a pink tissue. "Nanny will be back, but she'll need an assistant. The kids are getting so out of hand lately. Of course, you'll have to work very hard."

"Of course," Jacqui said, chewing the inside of her cheek.

"And have absolutely no distractions," Anna said meaningfully. "I have to insist on that. If you're going to be working for us during the school year, I expect you to be above reproach this summer." Anna glanced toward the door. "Do you understand what I'm saying?"

"I see." It slowly dawned on Jacqui what Anna was expecting from her in exchange for the job next year: Philippe.

"One other thing. I've decided to move Philippe into the main house. Zoë mentioned something about a particularly interesting game of pool she walked in on, and I really don't think we can have that kind of behavior around the children. Understood?"

A heavy, tension-filled silence settled on the room. Anna's laptop computer was the only sound for several seconds. Jacqui's mind raced with the implications of Anna's offer. On the one hand, Anna was offering her everything she was working toward that summer: a job, a place to stay, an opportunity to better herself. Yet on the other hand . . . there was Philippe. Philippe, with his sardonic grin, his angelic face, his bronzed, diesel-cut body. Philippe, the only guy since Luca who had set her blood pounding.

"Do you think you'll be able to manage?"

It was a bribe. An out-and-out bribe. *All right,* Jacqui thought grimly. If that was what it took, that was what it took. She would stop seeing Philippe. Never kiss him again. Never run her fingers through his soft hair. But, hey, there were other guys, right? One hot French guy wasn't worth her dream of moving to New York and going to college. No guy was worth her future.

She nodded. "Of course."

Anna Perry smiled. "I knew I could trust you."

the best things
in life are free?

WORKING AT A NIGHTCLUB WAS NOWHERE NEAR AS
glamorous as Eliza had expected it to be. Somehow even the ego
stroke of deciding who was going to get in and who was going to
have to call it a night didn't make up for all the humiliations that
catering to the celebrity and wannabe-celebrity clientele entailed.
The other night she'd had to spritz a famous actress's face with
Evian mist every fifteen minutes, since the actress didn't want her
skin to dehydrate while she downed magnums of champagne.

And it was the opposite of glamorous when she'd opened her
pay envelope and found out how much, exactly, she was actually
making while working at Seventh Circle. She had stormed into
Alan's office, insisting that a mistake had been made. Alan
glanced at her check. It appeared there *had* been a mistake—they
hadn't taken FICA taxes out, and the amount should have been
even less. Eliza did the math and realized she was barely clearing
minimum wage. When she complained to Kit, he told her that
when he'd interned at *Rolling Stone* one semester after school, he

hadn't been paid a dime. It was a prestige job, not a paying one. Eliza was privileged enough to work at Seventh Circle, and surely, since her parents were doing better, she didn't really need the money, right?

Except that she kind of did. Her parents had been generous enough to provide her the use of a MasterCard again, but after several trips to Calypso, Tracy Feith, and Georgina, she'd already maxed it out. She had to find a different stylish and sexy outfit to wear to work every night, and that was getting hard to do on a limited budget.

The job at Seventh Circle was supposed to be her entrée back into the good life, but instead of becoming an important fixture on the scene, like a junior Mitzi Goober, Eliza found herself catering to her former friends instead. The other day, she'd had to arrange for Sugar to bungee-jump off the top of the liquor cabinet—to the delight of her camera crew—and then sweep up the broken bottles she'd sent smashing to the floor.

Eliza arrived at the au pair cottage just in time to catch Mara and Jacqui counting the money in their pay envelopes. Philippe had already left for the weekend, citing an invitation from friends in Sag Harbor. Eliza felt a little ill seeing all that cash.

"Can we go to the bank?" Mara asked happily. If she spent one more summer working for the Perrys, she would have her entire college contribution covered.

Jacqui stuck her pay envelope into her bureau drawer carelessly, taking out several hundred-dollar bills just in case they went anywhere fun. She planned to use most of the money to pay for her SAT class, which was expensive but would hopefully be worth it.

"What's all this?" Eliza asked, noticing two rolling racks of clothes jammed in the corner. "Oh my God—are those the Sally Hershberger jeans?" Eliza squealed, pouncing on a pair of distressed denim jeans that retailed for one thousand dollars. "I want these," Eliza said covetously, holding the jeans up to the light and examining them closely. "How on earth did you get them?" she asked Mara.

"Mara's famous," Jacqui teased, rifling through the shopping bags and finding a pretty psychedelic Pucci scarf. It was true. Garrett Reynolds was the heir to a billion-dollar fortune, and the papers chronicled his love life with the same zeal with which they documented the spiraling construction costs of the Reynolds Castle. (The blueprints had recently been leaked to the press, revealing the home's thirty-five bathrooms.) Garrett's former girlfriends included actresses like Kate Bosworth and rock royalty like Keith Richards's model daughter Theodora. Mara's relatively obscure background made her even more of a choice subject to the press, especially Lucky Yap, who loved to run photos of the very public, very attractive couple. Page Six had nicknamed them "Beauty and the Billionaire Boy."

Mara blushed and explained in an apologetic tone that they were "gifts" from designers to wear around town.

"You mean these are free?" Eliza gasped. No wonder Mara had

looked so good the other night at Seventh Circle. Eliza's eyes widened as she pawed through the loot. The leopard-print Shoshanna cape! The latest Alvin Valley leather-band trousers! The turquoise-encrusted Marni dress! The two-thousand-dollar Devi Kroell python clutch!

"Wow, that is crazy," Eliza said. "I can't believe you have all these!"

The Sally Hershberger jeans! She'd been lusting for a pair ever since she read about them in Vogue. They were supposed to be the best jeans on earth, the softest, rarest European and Japanese denim cut by the hand by Sally Hershberger—the Hollywood stylist who charged six hundred dollars for a haircut.

"Do you think I could borrow them? We're the same size, right?" Eliza asked, pulling the jeans out and pressing them against her legs.

"Oh, I don't know," Mara said nervously. "I had to sign all these responsibility forms."

Eliza pouted. "That's only a formality. They really won't want these back ever. Right, Jac?"

Jacqui shrugged. "They usually let you keep them, but it depends, I guess."

Eliza had already stepped out of her cargos and zipped up the jeans. "They look amazing! I can't believe they sent them to *you*!" She said.

"Why not?" Mara asked, feeling a little hurt. Eliza hadn't come over to hang out with them all summer and now that she was here, she didn't seem to think Mara deserved the free clothes from Mitzi.

Eliza didn't answer. She was too excited to be wearing the jeans. "Can I borrow them? Please, please, please? With sugar on top?"

"Oh, all right," Mara said, caving in. "But if anything happens to them . . . !" she raked her thumb across her neck.

Eliza squealed and hugged Mara tightly. "I owe you!"

Mara still didn't feel it was totally right to lend Eliza clothes that weren't hers, but she didn't feel like she could really say no.

"So what's going on with you and Garrett?" Eliza asked, changing back into her own clothes. Jacqui handed Eliza a shopping bag for the jeans.

"I like him," Mara said hesitantly. "He's a cool guy. I thought he was just some obnoxious rich kid, but he's not."

"What about Ryan?" Jacqui asked.

"He doesn't even remember that I'm alive," Mara shrugged. The new, aloof Ryan was sure not the sweet boy she remembered from last summer. "So, I don't know. Who cares about him, right?"

Eliza felt relieved. It looked like she could stop worrying about Palm Beach. If Mara had moved on from Ryan, then who cared? Even Jacqui had stopped thinking it was a big deal. Like everyone else in the Hamptons, she'd started to think of Mara as Garrett Reynolds's new girlfriend.

Mara found an outpost of her bank, and after depositing her money met Eliza and Jacqui at the Neiman Marcus Last Call store at the outlet mall, where they were browsing through the discounted designer offerings. The place was famous for selling glamorous duds from seasons past at fire-sale prices. Price tags were stamped with color-coded stickers according to date, and the longer they remained unsold, the cheaper they became.

"Check it out!" Eliza giggled, holding up a minuscule orange tube top with a busy multicolored print. "Do you think it's too much?"

"It's definitely loud," Mara agreed.

"But it's Missoni," Eliza said reverently. "And in my size. I'm getting it. It's going to look great with my new jeans," she said, already feeling possessive of the Hershberger denim. She found several other choice pieces—a nifty little white Balenciaga coat dress that didn't look too last-season, and a Yves Saint Laurent lipstick-print skirt with a small black smudge that Eliza was sure a good dry cleaner could get out. Jacqui found a gray Narciso Rodriguez shift and a pair of Christian Dior sunglasses, both at less than half price.

"You're not getting anything?" Eliza asked Mara, as they walked up to the counter. "Did you see the Marc Jacobs flats back there?"

"I have the new ones," Mara said, wiggling her toes in a pair of the designer's bubble-gum-colored open-toed shoes.

"Oh," Eliza said, feeling a little strange that Mara of all people would be the one with the latest "it" garments. She had thought all along that being associated with Seventh Circle would bring her those kinds of perks, but so far, the only bounty she'd scored was a free movie pass to a screening Kartik wasn't interested in.

"I just have so many clothes at home that I haven't even worn yet," Mara sighed as she absently picked up an open perfume bottle near the counter and took a big sniff.

Did Mara not hear how snotty she sounded? "Yeah, I forgot, you're like, the Julia Roberts of the Hamptons," Eliza grumbled, even more ticked when her total at the cash register was more than what was left on her card. "Jac, do you think I could borrow a fifty?"

Jacqui shook her head while handing Eliza the money. Eliza would never change. Give the girl a million bucks and she would still be broke by midweek. Apparently looking like a million cost that much too. Unless you were Mara Waters, of course.

the world looks
better from atop a
pedestal (or a table)

"CAN WE GET ONE OF MARA ONLY?" THE PHOTOGRAPHERS demanded when Garrett and Mara stepped out of the Maybach at the entrance to Seventh Circle late on a Saturday night. Since the Fourth of July, which they'd spent together on the Reynoldses' boat watching fireworks burst above the Atlantic, the two of them had been inseparable.

"Be my guest," Garrett bowed, stepping aside. "She's something else, isn't she?" he asked, as Mara was blinded by flashbulbs.

"You are such a star," he growled in her ear as they settled into their usual table. Even though she'd initially gone out with Garrett only to make Ryan jealous, Mara couldn't help but enjoy his company.

He swung an arm around the back of the booth and put his hand possessively on her shoulder. She snuggled underneath his armpit, liking the feel of his heavy hand on her bare skin. Garrett leaned over for a kiss, settling in to nuzzle his cheek against her neck at the same moment she looked up from the table, straight into the eyes of Ryan Perry. He was standing next to Allison, who was waving to Garrett.

Garrett disengaged from Mara's cleavage. "Perry!" he said, throwing out a hand. "Hey, Ali. What are you doing with this bozo?" he joked.

Ryan shook Garrett's hand grimly. "Hi, Garrett. Mara."

"Hey," she said back. It was the most Ryan had said to her all week. Usually he'd just nod at her curtly if she bumped into him at the house.

Garrett stood up to kiss Allison on the cheek. "Sit down with us, c'mon."

Ryan raised his eyebrow to Allison, who shrugged and returned Garrett's smile. "Sure," she said, taking the seat next to Garrett.

Ryan was wearing a loose-fitting guayabera shirt and faded blue jeans, what he used to joke was "surfer black-tie." Garrett suddenly looked overdressed in his Dolce & Gabbana French-cuffed dress shirt and starchy dark denim jeans.

Mara disengaged herself from Garrett, but Ryan turned around and started talking only to Allison, who was giggling at something Garrett was whispering in her other ear. Garrett explained that he and Allison went to the same prep school back in New York, and soon, the three of them began talking about kids they knew in common.

"Did you hear about Fence Preston? He's about to blow up, for sure," Garrett was saying.

"You're so much cuter," Allison said, poking Ryan in the nose affectionately.

Mara, who had no idea who or what a Fence Preston was, felt nervous and neglected. But Garrett made sure to refill her glass whenever it was half-empty, and she began downing drinks with a vengeance.

"Let's do shots," Garrett suggested.

"Sure," Mara agreed.

Garrett ordered a bottle of Goldschläger and poured the clear liquid with golden sparkles into four glasses.

"This stuff is gross," Allison said daintily, taking a small sip and making a face.

Ryan grimly knocked his back. Mara, wanting desperately to impress him, did the same with hers. "Let's do another!" Garrett howled, and the three of them pounded back a few more.

It was right about the time that all four shots hit Mara that the DJ played his nightly remix of Bon Jovi's "Livin' on a Prayer." Seventh Circle regulars like Garrett and Mara recognized it as the Seventh Circle anthem. It was the song that officially kicked off the evening and was guaranteed to get the celebrities dancing on the tables.

"I looooove this song!" Mara howled, singing along. "This is awesome!"

"Isn't this the best?" Chauncey Raven asked, leaning over to their banquette. The petite pop star was wearing a black bra underneath a tight white T-shirt, and a denim mini with the hems slashed so high that the white pockets peeked out from underneath. She was barefoot, with a sparkly toe ring. "C'mon, let's dance!" she said, climbing up on their table and pulling Mara up to join her.

Feeling dizzy and exhilarated, Mara followed the pop star's lead, and the two of them gyrated hips and threw their hair around in a dazzling imitation of a cheesy eighties music video.

"You too!" Chauncey said, noticing Allison sitting down.

Allison shook her head, a bemused expression on her face. "Oh no, thanks, I prefer to do my dancing on chairs."

"Oh, I forgot my drink!" Chauncey said, hopping off in search of her cocktail glass.

Alone on top of the table, Mara accidentally kicked the bottle of Goldschläger to the side, and Ryan Perry saved it from crashing to the floor at the last minute. Mara froze for a moment, feeling vulnerable and exposed. She noticed that Ryan was looking at her strangely. Maybe she should get off the table. She hesitated—but then Garrett cheered at her.

"All right! *Go, Mara!*" he yelled, whooping it up. He was laughing and wolf whistling, and several other people in club turned to cheer as well. Inspired, she danced even more wildly. The banquette was soon bathed in the spotlight of photographers' flashbulbs.

"Over here!"

"Look this way, luv!"

"Over your shoulder, Mara!"

"Can we get one with you leaning over Garrett?"

Only too happy to oblige, Mara leaned over and gave Garrett a kiss on his forehead, sending the paparazzi into a frenzy as their cameras flashed. Mara slunk her hips, pouting and posing, noticing how Ryan couldn't take his eyes off her. Finally! He was looking at her!

"'*Woooooaaah, we're halfway there-uh. . . . Whoooahh, livin' on a prayah . . .*'" she sang. She was having the time of her life until she felt a hand on her ankle. She looked down. Eliza was glaring at her, looking pretty steamed for some reason. But Mara was nothing but delighted to see her.

"'Liza! Come up here!" she enjoined. "'*Take my hand, we'll make it I swear!*'" she sang, holding out her hand to her friend.

"Get down! Get down! Get down this minute!" Eliza hissed, pulling at her ankle.

"*What?* I can't hear you!" Mara shouted.

"We have a health inspector here tonight—this is a *restaurant*! You can't dance on the tables! They'll shut us down!"

"*What?*" Mara asked, laughing.

"I said, *get down*!!" Eliza screamed, "Oh my God, oh my God." She pulled Mara off the table, and Mara stumbled down, her skirt almost catching on the candle. She landed on Garrett's lap.

"What on earth were you thinking? I could get fired!" Eliza said angrily.

"What's wrong with you?" Mara demanded. It wasn't like Mara was doing anything different from what Lindsey Lohan had pulled the night before.

"Nothing's wrong with me—you're the one who's being a total brat," Eliza spat. Mara was acting just like the spoiled celebrities who thought they owned the place.

"Excuse me?" Mara yelped. "What did you call me?"

"Hey, hey, cool down," Ryan said, standing up and holding his arms out between the two seething girls. "Mara, Eliza didn't mean it."

"Shut up, Ryan!" Mara glared. "Who asked you?" It was just like Ryan to be on Eliza's side. Why couldn't he be on her side just for once? He was always defending Eliza. Even last summer, when she'd first met Eliza and Eliza had been such a witch to her, Ryan had told her not to hold it against Eliza since her family was going through some "hard times." As if Mara didn't know what hard times were like!

Meanwhile, Eliza noticed that Garrett was leaning against his chair, smirking and enjoying the show. He was probably thinking that if he was lucky enough, Mara and Eliza would start rolling around the floor, pulling each other's hair out in a proper cat-fight. Eliza was disgusted by him. For the first time, she wondered what Mara saw in him besides all that money.

"Mara, calm down," Eliza said. "You're drunk."

That only made Mara more furious. *Hello,* who was a bigger lush than Eliza? The girl practically lived on vodka-cranberries. "Um, excuse me, I'm in a nightclub!" Mara yelled, drunk and belligerent. "You're just jealous because I'm in the VIP room and you just work here!"

Eliza reacted as if slapped. "Stop acting like a bitch!"

"I'm a bitch? You're the one who's been acting so weird all summer!" Mara said, knowing it was true. Eliza had blown her off almost all summer and had been short with her when they had hung out.

They glared at each other. Last summer, the two of them had had a hard time seeing eye to eye, and they'd done their share of bickering. But this was so much worse.

"Oh God, I feel sick," Mara said, holding a hand to her mouth and clutching her stomach with the other. Then she leaned over and threw up all over Eliza's new Marc Jacobs shoes.

Before blacking out, the last thing Mara remembered was seeing a look of utter disgust on Ryan's face.

you'll always love
your first love

SEVENTH CIRCLE CLOSED AT 5 A.M., AND ELIZA PUNCHED her card and walked through the empty club to the staff rooms in the back. The fight with Mara had rattled her. Not only had she gotten yelled at by her bosses, since she'd barely gotten Mara down from the table before the health inspector saw what was going on, but her new shoes were ruined, and unlike Mara, she didn't have several free pairs waiting at home. She felt tired and defeated and a little resentful. How was it that *she*—Eliza Thompson, who used to run rampant through a slew of Manhattan nightclubs—was now the one who was dead sober at the end of the evening, with puke-covered shoes, no less?

She slid her feet from the mottled suede heels and put on a pair of flip-flops and a bulky Princeton sweatshirt that was as long as her skirt. The bar backs were hosing down the bar and the night porter had arrived to clear the garbage. She said good-bye to Milly, the coat-check girl, and split her tips with the three waitresses. They'd had a decent evening because Eliza had decided that names could magically appear on the list with the help of a hundred-dollar bribe. She had to supplement her meager income somehow.

"You're still here?" she asked, seeing Ryan Perry sitting alone by the bar.

He nodded. "What do you mean? I never leave," he joked. "Nah. I was waiting for you. Just wanted to make sure you get home safe."

"That's sweet," she said. She was glad they still had that easy connection and that their friendship was just the same as it was before.

"Want a drink? You look like you need one," Ryan offered.

"I'm the one who works here, remember? Johnnie? Could we have one for the road?" The bar back nodded and provided them with two glasses of whiskey.

"None for me, thanks," Ryan said.

"Well, then—I'll have yours too. Shame to let it go to waste," Eliza smiled, sipping her glass. "God, what was up with Mara tonight?"

"I have absolutely no idea," Ryan said, tapping his knuckles on the counter.

"Me either," Eliza said, raising her glass in a mock salute.

"I'll drive you home," he offered, when Eliza finished off the second tumbler.

"But—my car." Eliza motioned to her Jetta parked in the lot.

"I'll have Laurie send someone out to get it tomorrow," Ryan told her.

They drove with the top down on Ryan's car, and Eliza found herself telling him about how her job at Seventh Circle wasn't everything she'd thought it would be. She shook out a cigarette from her pack and lit it. "Want one?" she asked him. Ryan shook his head, then thought better of it. Eliza helped him light his cigarette, cupping it against the wind.

"Thanks," Ryan said, talking from the side of his mouth as he steered the car to the highway.

Eliza exhaled a huge plume of smoke. "And Jeremy hasn't even called me in two weeks," she complained. "I have no idea what's going on between us. He tells me he missed me all year, but then he like, drops off the face of the earth."

Ryan nodded in sympathy. Eliza put her bare feet up on the dashboard, feeling more relaxed and comfortable than she had in a long time. "So what's going on with you and Allison?" she asked.

"Not much." He shrugged. "I think she's into me, but we're just friends."

"Dude, everyone likes you," Eliza emphasized. "That's so not news."

He laughed and tapped the ashes from his cigarette in the wind. "I wish."

"Mara and Garrett look pretty cozy, huh?" Eliza noted, not to be mean, but just as an observation. "They're at the club together almost every night."

"I guess," Ryan shrugged. "She's different now."

When they arrived in front of Eliza's house, she hesitated before getting out of the car. "You want to maybe come in for a little bit?" she asked. "I'm so wired and I know I won't be able to sleep for a while yet. We could watch *Godfather Two.* . . ."

"Sure." Ryan shrugged. He didn't seem to want to be alone just yet either.

Ryan sat back on the couch, and Eliza tiptoed out of the kitchen holding a bowl of microwaved popcorn and two bottles of Diet Coke. She popped the DVD in. It was so natural, hanging out with Ryan. He'd been in the background all her life. She remembered how when they were little, their families used to vacation together in the Bahamas at Christmas. They'd learned to ski together on the slopes of Aspen. Eliza remembered Ryan's mom— his real mom, Brigitte—saying the two of them would make a good couple when they grew up. Back then, Sugar and Poppy were still called Susan and Priscilla, and they'd followed Eliza around like little puppies, competing with each other to be the one to brush her hair or be her ski-lift partner. The twins sure had changed, but Ryan was still the same—still here, still right next to her.

Robert De Niro was beating up some guys on the screen, and Eliza leaned back on the couch, nestling her head on Ryan's shoulder. But when Ryan leaned down to say something, their lips met instead. She didn't mean for it to happen, but instead of pulling away, Eliza opened her mouth to his. He pulled up her sweatshirt and began to unbutton her blouse, unhooking her bra, kissing every inch of her.

She was thinking it was wrong—that she should stop him— but it felt so . . . right. It was just like in Palm Beach, exactly like in Palm Beach—two broken hearts finding comfort in each other. That was all it was really, just hooking up. It didn't mean anything, she told herself.

And then she wasn't thinking of anything at all, because Ryan was kissing her again, and whatever worries she had, whatever doubts about where this was headed (nowhere, she thought), and what it would mean (nothing, she hoped) were made completely irrelevant by the sweet insistence of his lips on hers.

the doctor is
definitely out

"WHERE'S MARA?" ZOË ASKED WHEN JACQUI ARRIVED
to get the kids ready the next morning.

"She's sick," Jacqui said grimly, helping the little girl tie her
bathrobe. "It's only me, okay?" Mara had certainly looked green
around the gills that morning. Mara had overslept again, and
when Jacqui tried to wake her, she'd mumbled something about a
killer hangover, which was turning into a frequent excuse.
Philippe was gone on another errand for Anna, and Mara and
Jacqui had agreed that if Jacqui dealt with the kids yesterday,
Mara would take the kids today so Jacqui could study for her
SATs. But of course, Mara had flaked again.

"Where's Philippe? Where's Philippe?" William asked, alter-
nately bouncing on his sneakers and gliding on the built-in
wheels. Jacqui cursed whoever had invented the damn things—
they made William twice as fast and harder to catch.

"I'm not sure," Jacqui said. "I think your mom needed him to
do something for her in the city again." Laurie had told her that

some French papers Anna wanted translated needed a few more corrections. It sounded incredibly fishy. Since agreeing to Anna's ultimatum, she had kept away from Philippe as directed, which was a little hard to do since every time Philippe caught her alone in the house, he wanted to know when he could see her again. He'd even accused her of playing hard-to-get, which Jacqui found ironic.

"*I told you, she's not my mom!*" William shouted in a deafening tone.

"Okay! Okay! Calm down, please!" Jacqui said. "*Merda!*" she cursed when she realized she'd forgotten to put swimming diapers on Cody. The regular ones weren't waterproof.

"Madison, are you coming with us today?" Jacqui asked. For the past month Madison had been standoffish with the au pairs, since they were technically not responsible for her anymore.

"I'm meeting a friend there," Madison nodded. She was perfectly turned out in a pink bathing suit and a velour cover-up and was primping with a mascara wand in the mirror.

"That's a lot of makeup for the beach, don't you think?" Jacqui asked, amused.

"That bikini's a little revealing, don't you think?" Madison snapped back, applying a deep berry lip gloss.

Jacqui felt a little hurt. She'd bonded with Madison last summer, and this year the child was a little beeyatch. And her stepmother didn't seem to care that the eleven-year-old walked around looking like a little tramp.

"It just gets a little hot on the beach, and it's bad for your skin," Jacqui said gently.

"I don't care," Madison declared.

Jacqui folded up Cody's stroller. He was getting way too big for it; his legs almost came up to his chin when he sat in it. The "baby" was four years old and he still preferred to ride rather than walk. Just yesterday, when she'd wheeled him out on Main Street, several women had asked her if her boy was "special," i.e., crippled. "Nope, just lazy!" Jacqui had said cheerfully.

For all of Anna's hypervigilance about the kids' diets, academic goals, and spirituality, Jacqui had never seen kids who were so lacking in the basics.

As she ushered them to the garage, they bumped into Dr. Abraham, walking out of a guest suite and munching on a banana. "We're off to the beach today? Hold on!" he said, and before Jacqui could disagree, the doctor ran out of his room carrying his tote bag.

"Looks like I have you all to myself," Dr. Abraham joked, seeing that Mara and Philippe were nowhere in sight.

"If you count the kids as nobody," Jacqui retorted.

The only car left in the lot was the tiny little Toyota Prius, and between Cody's car seat and the doctor's girth, it was a bit of a tight squeeze. Jacqui drove them to nearby Georgica, where the kids dispersed—Madison to look for her friends, William to run up and down the boardwalk, and Zoë to collect seashells.

"Don't go far! Only where I can see you!" Jacqui called out as she planted her beach umbrella and spread out her towel. She tied her hair back with the Pucci scarf Mara had told her she could borrow.

She stepped out of her cotton sundress and ignored the doctor's stares. She hoped that he would get the message and leave her alone.

The SAT tutorial was a little hard to follow—they'd gone over the verbal part of the exam at the class she'd missed to play pool with Philippe the other week. Jacqui just didn't get the word problems. Rock is to mountain as feather is to A) wing, B) chickens, C) pillow, or D) all of the above. In Portuguese, *rock* also meant "foundation" as well as "soil." In that case, the answer could be A, since wings were made out of feathers—but then, feathers were also the foundation of most pillows, which pointed to C. It was all very confusing.

"Man, that is a boring book!" a voice said from above her.

Jacqui looked up from under her floppy Panama hat and grinned. "Hey, Kit, how are you?"

"I'm good. A little bummed you didn't call the minute you got into town, but I lived," Kit Ashleigh joked, taking a seat next to her. He had a spiky blond crew cut, and he was so pale his nose was already peeling from the sun. He was one of Eliza's best friends, and Jacqui had gotten to know him better in Palm Beach. She knew Kit sort of had a crush on her, but she played it down. She liked Kit—but not in that way. Besides, there was her No More Boys rule, and so long as she was being forced to make it apply to Philippe, it had to apply to Kit as well.

"I'm sorry. It's been so busy, with the kids. . . . I haven't had a day off," Jacqui apologized.

"Who's the dork?" Kit asked, referring to the doctor, who was snoring underneath a paperback copy of Dr. Phil's *Family First*.

"A *falsificação* . . . like a . . . duck doctor?" Jacqui had a hard time with American slang.

"Quack?" Kit asked helpfully.

Jacqui nodded excitedly. "Exactly!" Leaning down, she whispered, "I hate him."

Kit nodded. "Let's ditch him," he said conspiratorially.

"What do you have in mind?" Jacqui asked, one finely plucked eyebrow raised.

is mara the new tara?

MARA WOKE UP WITH NO MEMORY OF WHAT HAD happened the night before. Her head was pounding, and she was so thirsty she walked to the bathroom and drank water straight from the faucet, cupping it with her hands. Lately, Mara was always waking up this way. It was almost noon, and as usual, Jacqui and the kids were already gone. She took a long shower, dried her hair, put on her most comfortable outfit—a terry zip-up hoodie swim cover-up—and hid her eye bags under a pair of sleek Oliver Peoples aviator sunglasses, all courtesy of the Mitzi gravy train.

She walked toward the main house, noticing there was a new addition to the Reynolds Castle that morning: a pair of giant armored knight statues that stood guard at the gates. She walked to the kitchen and made herself a smoothie and was rinsing out the blender when the newspaper caught her eye. She leafed through the *Post*, going straight to her favorite gossip column, Page Six. That's when she saw it.

"Oh my God." She clamped her hands to her mouth and looked around nervously. She looked at the photo again. *Oh my God.* Suddenly, images from last night began flooding back, making her head pound harder. Dancing on the table. Yelling at Ryan. Calling Eliza a bitch. But even worse—that awful picture in the paper!

She'd thought Lucky Yap was her friend. Some kind of friend he turned out to be. There it was, right in the middle of the Page Six column—underneath the headline *THE NEW TARA REID?* was a photo of her from last night. Mara Waters, the nice girl from Sturbridge—or at least that was how she'd always thought of herself—hanging over Garrett, his nose in her cleavage, her boobs literally *popping* out of her Gucci corset. Good Lord, one nipple had actually escaped from the tight bodice of the neckline!

Mortified didn't even begin to describe her feelings that morning. It was one thing to lose control for an evening and quite another to have it broadcast around the world. Mara hurriedly stuffed the newspaper into the garbage can, hoping nobody would see it. Especially not Ryan. It was just too embarrassing. *The new Tara Reid?* Even Tara Reid didn't want to have Tara Reid's reputation.

Mara blushed. A little part of her had always felt that even though the Perrys were wildly rich and privileged, there was nothing to be envious of, because they didn't have what she had—a great, solid family, with parents who had instilled in their three daughters the importance of integrity, honesty, and decency. But with the publication of that photo, she didn't have a leg to stand on. Neither Sugar nor Poppy had ever been captured in such a compromising position, although there had been that close call with Sugar's ex-boyfriend, who'd videotaped one of their steamy encounters. But Kevin's law firm and a hefty bribe had made that go away. Maybe Mara had been wrong about herself. Maybe she was just like everyone in the Hamptons—someone who'd do anything for attention and fame.

"Mara, didn't you hear me? There's someone at the door for you," Laurie said, walking into the kitchen.

Mara froze, feeling apprehensive. She wasn't expecting anyone. Was it against the law to get your photo taken? Were the nipple police here to get her? But when she opened the door, it was only a brown-uniformed messenger. "Sign here!" he said, pushing a clipboard under her nose.

She scribbled her name, and he thrust several oversize shopping bags into her arms. The bags contained three more gorgeous Shoshanna dresses, as well as a selection of pastel cashmere cardigans. Mara finally found a handwritten note on expensive cardstock stationery: *Excellent coverage in the* Post! *Keep it up! Hugs, Mitzi.*

The errant nipple aside, Mara understood that in Mitzi's view, the photo was a roaring success. The article in Page Six had named every brand she was wearing.

She gathered the bags just in time to see Ryan Perry pull up to the driveway. She froze, rooted to the spot. He climbed out of his car and walked toward her. He was bleary-eyed and still wearing the same clothes from the night before. Against her resolve, Mara's heart sank.

"Oh, er . . . hi, Mara," Ryan nodded, turning crimson.

"Morning." She nodded. It was so obvious he'd hooked up with somebody last night. Mara felt sickeningly jealous. It seemed that Ryan Perry would never lack for a girl in his life, and even worse, she would never be that girl again.

happiness is a full
sail on a strong wind

THERE WERE MANY ADVANTAGES TO KNOWING KIT
Ashleigh—his sense of humor, his steadfast loyalty to his friends, his many expensive playthings. But the one that was most important was his ability to have fun, no matter where he was. Kit was instrumental in rounding up all the kids, convincing William he'd let him steer the sailboat, letting Madison bring her friend, telling Zoë they would see dolphins, and carrying Cody to the car. They all piled into his Mercedes-Benz CLK convertible (Jacqui had left the keys to the Toyota underneath the doctor's suntan oil), and he drove them to Sag Harbor, where his sailboat was docked.

"It's really not much," Kit said of the Sunfish. "But it'll fit all of us, and maybe we can get the kids to learn how to sail. My dad taught me when I was a kid."

"This is it?" William asked, not impressed with the fifteen-foot craft. "My dad's is, like, three times as big."

"It's not all about size, my friend," Kit said, unfurling the sails and unhitching the ropes. "C'mon, give me a hand with this. You too, Madison, Zoë—everyone can help."

With Kit giving directions, they were able to cast off, and Kit steered them up to the dock next to the JLX Bistro, a trendy French restaurant on the water.

A waiter came right up to the boat and took their order, and a few minutes later, several bulging bags of cheese, prosciutto sandwiches, Caprese salads, and bottles of sparkling water and cider were passed over on the starboard side.

Jacqui was impressed. Kit steered them back out to sea.

"Can't we go any faster?" William whined.

"Here, let me show you," Kit said, jumping up. They caught a breeze and everyone was quiet. The water was calm and smooth, and the sailboat ran swiftly over the waves. It was a relaxing and thrilling at the same time. Jacqui unwrapped their picnic lunch, passing around the sandwiches.

"God, this is so queer," Madison's friend Angelica complained. "We should have stayed on Georgica. Those cute guys my cousin knows were supposed to be there today."

Madison, who seemed to be enjoying the ride so far, hastily agreed.

"You're not going to eat that, are you?" Angelica asked, as Madison spooned a slice of tomato and mozzarella onto her plate.

Madison quickly put it back.

Jacqui watched the exchange silently. She wanted to say some-

156

thing to Madison about how girls like Angelica, who were too skinny and privileged for their own good, just masked their own insecurities by making fun of everyone else, but she knew she would just embarrass the girl, so she kept her mouth shut.

Instead, Jacqui heaped her own plate with cheese, salami, bread, and pickled vegetables, and made a show of eating every last bite, to the fascination of both preteen girls, who couldn't believe anyone who looked like Jacqui could eat like that.

Angelica had already tried flattery to get Jacqui to like her, but since Jacqui hadn't responded, the girl had taken to calling Jacqui "the au pair" in a snotty voice. Jacqui was relieved when the two decided to make the most of the day and sunbathe quietly on the deck.

Jacqui looked around at the kids, who were all entertained, and at the glittering water and bright sun. She leaned back on the deck and felt the wind in her hair. She was glad to have a friend like Kit.

it's so much easier to lie on the phone

ELIZA DABBED A SPLOTCH MORE FOUNDATION ON HER neck. The hickeys from Ryan had bloomed overnight. She looked war-ravaged, with little purple and yellow love marks all over her chest, collarbone, and underneath her chin. It was more than a little distressing. She couldn't go to work looking like she'd just been mauled, hence the bottle of Bobbi Brown foundation. Thank God for perfect-blend makeup.

Okay, so that was a little weird—hooking up with Ryan again like that. What about Jeremy? Was she cheating on him or something? Were they even together? Eliza felt confused and a little sad. And Ryan—what was up with that? She didn't like Ryan, did she? Ryan was like, her friend. Like, her brother—okay, so not like her brother *exactly*.

That morning, he'd woken her up and carried her to her bed. "I gotta go. I don't think your parents will be so thrilled if they see us in the living room," he whispered, kissing her nose.

"Okay." She'd nodded sleepily.

"See you later," he said, tucking her in.

Eliza smiled at the memory, dabbing a smidge more green-tinted concealer to mask a hickey, when her cell rang.

"Hi, 'Liza, it's me."

"Oh," she said, holding a compact powder in midair. Mara. Shit. Had Ryan told her something?

"Listen . . ." Mara started.

Eliza sucked in her stomach.

"I'm really, really sorry about last night," Mara said. "I don't know what got into me. I've never been that drunk before."

"Oh." Eliza exhaled. "It's nothing—don't worry about it."

"I just want you to know I would never ever do anything to get you in trouble," Mara said. "I know how much your job means to you."

"No, really, seriously, don't worry about it," Eliza said, wanting nothing more than to hang up. Mara was being so nice, it was hard to take. It would be so much easier if Mara was a real bitch, but she wasn't.

"Well, I really feel awful about it," Mara insisted. "And in front of Ryan, too!"

"Mar—I really gotta go," Eliza said, cutting her off. Even though she and Ryan had agreed that last night was a fluke, just as Palm Beach had been, and nothing whatsoever was going on between them *at all*, Eliza couldn't deal with the guilt. Even if Mara had Garrett Reynolds now, it didn't make Eliza feel any better.

"Oh, okay. Maybe we can go get coffee later this week or something?" Mara asked meekly.

"Yeah, I'll call you, 'kay?" Eliza replied quickly.

"Okay," Mara answered, but Eliza was already stabbing at the END button.

Mara hung up the phone in the kitchen, feeling blue. Eliza was still totally pissed off, she could tell. She opened the patio doors and was surprised to see Philippe sun-bathing on a raft in the middle of the pool, smoking as usual. She'd thought he'd gone away to the city. He was supposed to be one of the au pairs, but they rarely saw him since he'd been relocated to the main house.

"Your sister called earlier," he said, tapping his ashes into the water. "Laurie was looking for you."

"Which one?"

Philippe shrugged.

It had to be Megan. Maureen had three kids and was too busy to call. Mara wondered why Megan hadn't phoned her cell, but then, she didn't get a great signal in the Hamptons. Mara went back to the kitchen and dialed Megan's number at work.

"Hey, Meg? It's me," Mara said.

"Mara! Our star!" The cheerful voice of her sister vibrated down the line.

"Oh my God. You saw it? The *Post*?"

"Of course I saw it. Hello, it's Meg you're talking to, remember? I saw you in *Us Weekly* the other day, too. You look cuter on

Page Six. A little risqué, but cute," Megan said authoritatively. Mara could hear the sounds of blow-dryers and scissors clicking in the background.

"You really think I looked good? Did Mom and Dad see it?" Mara asked, looking out the window where Philippe was floating in circles. Anna Perry walked out to the terrace, wearing a white bikini and transparent high heels. She stepped gingerly into the pool, and Philippe helped her situate herself on a similar raft. They glided to the other end, where the water spilled over to a waterfall and a Jacuzzi.

"Mara, are you listening?" Megan asked.

"Oh, no, sorry," Mara said. "What did you say?"

"I told you that I hid the paper from them—if they'd seen it, you'd be back home in like, ten seconds. You know what Dad's like."

"Thank God. I owe you."

"No kidding. That's why I'm coming down to visit you in two weeks. I want to see where my famous little sister hangs out!"

"That would be awesome!" Mara replied.

"I know. That's why I didn't wait for an invitation," Megan said.

"What do you mean? You know you're always welcome!" Mara protested.

"That's why I'm coming to visit. Anyway, I gotta go. I was supposed to rinse Mrs. Norman ten minutes and now her hair is going to be lavender. See you soon!"

Mara hung up the phone, feeling better. Her favorite sister,

Megan, was coming down to visit! It would be so great to have Megan around—they could do some normal stuff, like get burgers at O'Malley's in East Hampton and maybe have a lobster boil on the beach. Mara could use a little break, and there was nothing like family to bring you back down to earth when you've had too much champagne.

garrett reels in
a catch

THE RICH WERE DIFFERENT. MARA HAD UNDERSTOOD THAT ever since last summer, when she met the Perry twins, who didn't think anything of spending eight hundred dollars on a designer dress but drew the line at paying for their own cocktails, and Ryan Perry, who drove a custom-made British sports car but filled the tank with unleaded to save a few bucks. Only a family like the Reynoldses would build a saltwater pool—a giant fish tank you could swim in—a mere thirty feet from the ocean. Garrett invited Mara over to check it out, since it had just been stocked with fish. The water was warm and soothing as Mara stepped inside.

"Another one?" Garrett asked, wading in with a pitcher of mango margaritas.

"I've already had two," Mara said, waving it away. "Maybe I should cool it a little," she said. "My sister's coming to visit soon, I don't want her to think—"

"Think what?" he asked, drinking straight from the pitcher and smacking his lips.

It was a beautiful warm night, and the crickets were chirping.

"I don't know, like I'm some kind of party girl or something. I do have a job, you know," she reminded him. "What if the kids saw me in Page Six?" she agonized.

"You know what? You shouldn't worry so much. It's just a photo in a newspaper. You know what people do with the newspaper?" Garrett asked, waving the pitcher around, accidentally sloshing its contents into the pool.

Mara shook her head, wondering if the alcohol would hurt the fish.

"They throw it away at the end of the day. In London, they wrap french fries in it to soak up the oil!" He laughed and set the pitcher by the side of the pool. He swam up, splashing her with water. "I like you, Mara. You're fun. Be *fun!*"

Mara glowed. He liked her. He'd said it out loud. With his hair all wet, he looked so cute, like a sleek, dark seal. He smiled at her, and she touched his face, liking how nonjudgmental he was. Ryan Perry probably thought she was the biggest hoochie in the Hamptons, but Garrett Reynolds thought she was fun.

A school of orange-and-white clown fish darted around the nearby coral, and Mara refilled her glass. It was delicious, and besides, hadn't Megan wanted to come to the Hamptons to experience all the glamour? Who wanted to go get lobster rolls in Montauk when you could hang out in the VIP room at Seventh Circle with movie stars?

Garrett threw her a pair of goggles and a snorkel and

switched on the underwater lights. She dipped her head underneath and looked around. The water was a bright, cerulean blue, as clear as daylight, and populated by colorful sea creatures of every size and shape. There were sea turtles and moray eels, brilliantly stark zebra fish, angelfish, rainbow fish, and blue-finned emperor fish.

"This is amazing," she told him, stopping to take the snorkel out of her mouth.

"Why go to St. Barths when you can bring St. Barths to you?" Garrett asked, adjusting his goggles. "That's the problem with the Hamptons: there's no good scuba."

A school of black stingrays floated by their knees. Mara watched them glide toward the reef, marveling at their smooth and graceful pace.

Garrett held her hand as they floated across the pool, pointing out transparent jellyfish and pulsating starfish. He swam toward an imitation grotto, a man-made cavern in the middle of the pool, and gestured to Mara to follow.

Mara held her cocktail above the waves, ducking into the cave. She'd thought the Perrys lived well, but this was a whole other level entirely. The Reynolds house was like Versailles and, well, SeaWorld all rolled into one.

"This is my favorite spot," Garrett said, pulling her closer to him. "Have you ever been to Capri?"

Mara shook her head. Apart from the Hamptons, she'd never really been anywhere.

melissa de la cruz

He wrapped his arms around her waist and pulled her closer. "Some day I'll take you there," he whispered in her ear.

"Mmmm," Mara smiled, liking the idea of that.

She wondered what Ryan was doing right then, but shook the thought out of her mind.

The dark cavern made Garrett's dark hair gleam with blue-black highlights, and his eyes glittered with mischief. "Bet you can't hold your breath underwater longer than I can," he challenged.

"Oh, ho! Bet I can!" Mara disagreed.

Mara inhaled and bent down, puffing her cheeks with oxygen, determined to prove him wrong. Garrett reached out to hold her hand as they sank underneath the water. Then he was kissing her, breathing into her mouth, salty and slick, hot and wet, and Mara surrendered to the novel sensation of being electrified by his touch, because for the longest time, she hadn't thought anyone but Ryan could make her feel that way again.

do two kind-of boyfriends equal one whole one?

EVERY SUMMER SINCE ELIZA COULD REMEMBER, THE Meadow Club in Southampton held an amateur tennis tournament for its members. Over the years, the two-day event had grown from a private, low-key country club match to one of the most important stops on the tennis circuit, complete with an official corporate sponsor, and had since been dubbed the Rolex Invitational. The tourney was able to attract tennis stars like Andy Roddick and Lindsay Davenport, as well as former luminaries like Pete Sampras and Ivan Lendl, to compete for the grand prize, a silver plate and a ten-thousand-dollar check. However, this year, none of the players were famous or internationally ranked, much to the chagrin of the club, which counted on the publicity the stars garnered.

At the end of the week, everyone turned out to watch the men's and women's championships. A well-heeled crowd in Lacoste polos and cheerful madras prints watched as

Philippe double faulted against his opponent, a hulking Swede.

Jacqui sat in the back with the kids, whom she'd bribed with ice cream bars. She knew how badly Philippe wanted to win the championship, but this was not going well. In the front box, Jacqui noticed Anna Perry watching the game with interest as well. Even though Jacqui knew she had to stay away from Philippe, there was something about watching Anna watch him that made her want him more. She still remembered the way he'd kissed her on the pool table. As much as she tried, Jacqui couldn't shake the memory.

On the adjoining court, Eliza was matching a two-time NCAA champ from Stanford serve for serve. She'd won the semifinal in a nail-biting sudden-death round, and it was a total thrill to be in the finals. She'd never expected this. Eliza looked up at the stands, enjoying being the center of attention for the first time all summer. She caught Ryan's eye and smiled at him in the front row, and then looked up again and saw Jeremy. She botched her serve, lobbing it into the net weakly.

Mara was sitting in the front box next to Garrett, directly opposite from Ryan, but she and Ryan weren't looking at each other. Sugar and Poppy were there as well, close to Mara. Eliza noticed that the three girls were wearing identical pastel Cynthia Rowley dresses. Totally weird—they'd hardly known Mara existed last summer.

Eliza shook the distractions from her head. This was it: last set. The Stanford champ sent a liner down the middle. Eliza sent it back with a powerful crash. Game. Set. Match. And just like that, Eliza won.

The NCAA champ was giving interviews in the locker room, trying to explain away her loss to a high school student, so Eliza ducked in, took a quick shower, and changed into a tiny Sabbia Rosa camisole and white Chloé jeans. She ran out to the hallway, hoping to avoid her surly opponent.

"Hey, good game!"

Eliza looked around. Ryan was standing underneath the archway with a bouquet of flowers.

"Ryan! Thanks!" She smiled, flushed and happy to see him. "Are those for me?"

Ryan handed the flowers over and they hugged warmly. Ryan was leaning down to kiss Eliza on the cheek when another hand tapped her on the shoulder. She turned to find Jeremy, smiling a little warily at her.

"Hey!" Eliza enthused, throwing her arms around Jeremy's neck.

"You were great on that court," Jeremy whispered.

Eliza smiled into Jeremy's polo shirt, almost forgetting that he'd completely blown her off ever since dinner with her parents. Ryan coughed, and Eliza remembered her manners.

"Jeremy, you know Ryan Perry, right? He's an old friend of mine," Eliza explained, a little nervously.

"Sure. I used to work for you guys," Jeremy said, taking Ryan's hand.

"How are you, man?" Ryan asked. The two of them clenched hands, smiling tightly at each other. Ryan affected a relaxed pose that Eliza could tell was just an act.

"Oh, Eliza, this is Carolyn," Jeremy said, turning to introduce a tall, auburn-haired girl behind him. "Eliza Thompson, Carolyn Flynn."

Eliza handed Ryan the bouquet so she could shake hands with Jeremy's friend.

"You should turn pro," Carolyn said. "That was amazing."

"Thanks—you're sweet. You know, you look familiar," Eliza said, narrowing her eyes. "You went to Spence, didn't you?"

"I think I was a year older," Carolyn agreed.

"And you two know each other?" Eliza asked, gesturing from Carolyn to Jeremy.

"We're both interning at Morgan," Jeremy explained.

Eliza felt her jaw muscles tighten from having to smile so much. It was so great to see Jeremy—finally. And she was so touched he'd actually remembered the tennis tournament, but it sort of seemed like he was here . . . with a date.

"I'm sorry I haven't been by the club," Jeremy was saying. "Work has been killer."

"That's okay," Eliza said. "Make it up to me tonight at Seventh Circle?"

He nodded. "I'll be there."

"Me too," said Ryan, still holding the bouquet of flowers, but Eliza was already gone.

forbidden love is the greatest aphrodisiac

JACQUI RAPPED ON THE DOOR. SHE KNEW PHILIPPE was sulking inside. Having lost the game in the most humiliating manner—6–0, 6–0, 6–3—he had stormed off the court. But watching Anna watch him at the game, Jacqui decided that she might just want to help him feel . . . better. She opened the door and walked in, just as Anna Perry was walking out.

"Oh! Excuse me!" Jacqui said. "I was just—"

"The children's wing is that way, Jacqui," Anna said in a cold voice.

"Yes, I . . . I was just looking for Cody's blanket," Jacqui said, hurrying away. She ran down the hallway, and when Anna's footsteps receded, she tiptoed quickly back to Philippe's door.

"Hurry, open up, it's me," she whispered.

"It's open," he whispered back.

She walked in to find Philippe lying on his bed, smoking a cigarette and looking a little more relaxed than he had earlier when he'd thrown his racket against the concrete and pushed away the TV cameras.

"What was that about?" she asked.

"What?" Philippe replied.

"Anna." Jacqui motioned over her shoulder.

"Who?"

"Our boss. Was she just with you?"

Philippe shrugged.

Jacqui pressed her lips tightly together. Looking at Philippe now, completely sweaty from the match, his honey blond hair damp and stuck to his handsome face, she could hardly resist him. Knowing she wasn't supposed to be with him made her want him even more. But if he really was having an affair with Anna Perry, then that was another story.

"Don't worry about Anna Perry," Philippe said, practically reading her mind. "It's not your concern. Can I help it if she is attracted to me? But me, I am not attracted to her, so there is nothing between us."

"That's not what I was thinking," Jacqui lied.

Philippe took a drag from his cigarette, letting the smoke whirl around them. "Really." He smiled.

Jacqui smiled back. God, he was hot. "Well, how are you feeling? Are you okay?" she asked gently.

"It's just a game," he said, stubbing out his cigarette and readjusting his head against a pillow.

"Well, I'm sorry." Jacqui looked at the door, nervous that Anna would come back at any minute.

"I'm sorry too," Philippe said. "But as Americans say, you win some, you lose some, *n'est-ce pas?*" He smiled impishly. "What are you doing here, anyway?" he asked. "I have to lose a tennis match to get your attention?"

"Well, you've been kind of busy with someone else," Jacqui said, sitting down on the side of the bed.

"Anna Perry again! What do I have to do to make you believe there is nothing between me and that woman?" Philippe asked, throwing up his arms.

"Prove it," Jacqui taunted, her full lips parting into a sexy smile.

Philippe pulled her toward him. "Is this what you want?" he asked, between kisses.

Jacqui responded by kissing him ardently back. He slid his hand up the back of her shirt, but she pushed him away. "No—not now . . ." she said, looking at the door again.

"When?" Philippe asked.

"We'll figure something out," Jacqui said, smoothing her hair and kissing him one last time.

She stuck her head out the door. The coast was clear. She ran out the door, just as Dr. Abraham was walking purposefully toward his room. As she shuffled down the hallway toward the kids' wing, Jacqui heard them talking and wondered what that was all about. Philippe was one popular boy.

mara acquires a perry
sister nickname

NEVER JUDGE A BOOK BY ITS COVER. THAT WAS WHAT MARA had always been taught, growing up in a small town like Sturbridge. Her parents were heavily into clichéd sayings, such as *Still waters run deep* and *The Lord helps those who help themselves*, which her mother had embroidered and framed in their kitchen. For the most part, Mara abided by the first one—she was always willing to give people a second chance.

Look at Garrett Reynolds. She'd assumed he was some rich playboy who only had one thing on his mind, but he'd turned out to be genuinely interested in her. So, she'd been wrong about Garrett. Could it be possible she'd been wrong about Poppy and Sugar as well?

It had started innocently enough, when she and Garrett had attended Charlie Borshok's birthday party, at Sugar's invitation. They'd had a decent time, and the twins hadn't mentioned one thing about her being an au pair. In fact, unlike last summer, they were treating her like one of them. Poppy, who'd recently come back from a "spa" in Arizona with a pumped-up chest and her hair dyed dark chocolate brown, was especially friendly after the Nipplegate incident. "It's good to be a little controversial—it keeps people interested," she'd told Mara.

Poppy knew all about controversy. Since she had been overlooked by the reality show, Poppy had tried to recapture the spotlight through alternative means. First up: a line of scented candles inspired by her oh-so-glamorous life. Fragrances included New York City Musk, which unfortunately smelled exactly like its name; Last Call, which smelled like the backroom of a bar; and Fame, made from poisonous elderberries and cloyingly sweet gardenias. It didn't seem to bother their parents that neither of the twins was planning on going back to high school in the fall. As Sugar put it, they could always get their GEDs just like everybody else in Hollywood.

The night of the launch party for Sniffers by Poppy Perry at Seventh Circle, Poppy had totaled the family's Mercedes SUV. Kevin had not been pleased and had told the girls that they could either drive the Volvo or pay for a new car themselves. Unwilling to raid their own trust funds, the twins had asked Mara if she'd mind if they joined her in that sweet little 7-series BMW convertible she was tooling around town in.

They were the last two girls on earth that Mara had ever thought she would like—but since they were invited to all the same parties and were friends with Garrett's friends, and there was no one else for Mara to hang out with anyway, it just seemed natural. Even though Eliza had told Mara not to worry about it, Mara and Eliza hadn't hung out since that night at Seventh Circle. Mara was upset that Eliza was harboring a grudge, but she didn't know how to resolve their quarrel.

Later that evening, Mara was sitting on Sugar's platform bed, the three of them trying on clothes and putting on makeup.

"This is gorgeous," Mara said, fingering a daringly low-cut white Versace dress in Sugar's closet.

"I know, it's like, my fave," Sugar said. "I can't wear it anymore, though. It's been in too many magazines. And I'd give it to Pop, but it won't fit her anymore because of, you know"—she laughed, pointing at her sister's chest—"the surgery."

"Shut up! They still *huuuurt*," Poppy whined, rubbing her breasts. "Mara, you try it on," Poppy encouraged. "I bet it'll look amazing on you. C'mon."

"I couldn't!" Mara said, although she was already stepping out of her shorts and pulling up the dress over her hips.

"What are you wearing tonight?"

"I hadn't decided." Mara said, zipping up the white Versace.

"Oh my God. Poppy, look!"

"Oh. My. God."

"What?" Mara asked, "Does it look stupid?"

Poppy turned Mara to the full-length mirror. "Doesn't she look like a ripe, juicy, perfectly sweet little plum?" she asked her sister.

"Totally," Sugar drawled. "She is *such* a plum."

"Plum—that's it! Your new name! That's what we're going to call you from now on. No offense, but 'Mara' is so boring," Poppy said with her hand on her hip.

"That dress is made for you. You know what? You look so good in it, you should keep it," Sugar told her grandly.

Poppy nodded enthusiastically. "You look like that Russian model Natalia Something!"

"Really? You think so?" Mara blushed. She looked at herself in the mirror. It was the same dress Eliza had worn to P. Diddy's birthday bash last year, and Mara remembered wondering where Eliza had gotten it. Now she knew.

"Darling, it's yours. A present," Sugar said. "Anything for our Plum."

"Hey, do you guys know if Ryan is seeing anyone?" Mara asked, suddenly. She'd noticed that Allison had stopped coming over to the house lately.

Sugar shrugged, and Poppy looked blank.

"Not that we know of," Sugar assured, winking at Poppy when Mara turned around.

"C'mon, we gotta go to the club," Poppy said. "I'll drive," she declared, jangling Mara's BMW keys.

Eliza stood outside the club, manning her little four-foot-square empire, shivering in yet another skimpy outfit. She recognized the BMW that pulled up, but why was Poppy driving it? Poppy threw the keys to the valet, and Sugar slid out of the passenger side. The twins posed for a few shots, completely ignoring Eliza in order to squeal hellos to Kartik.

"Hey, wait up!"

Eliza turned to see Mara climb out of the back door of her car, running unevenly after the twins. Eliza grabbed Mara's arm as she walked past. "What, we don't say hello anymore?"

"Eliza! I didn't see you!" Mara squealed, in pitch-perfect imitation of Sugar's signature greeting. "Congratulations on the win today. You rocked!"

"Plum! Get your ass over here!" Poppy yelled from the entrance to the club.

"Coming!" Mara screeched, running over. "Bye-yee!"

Plum? Eliza wondered. Who the hell was *Plum?* Eliza stared at Mara's retreating back. Was she just imagining things, or was Mara wearing Sugar's white Versace dress? *In front of Sugar?*

As Eliza watched, dark-haired Mara and newly brunette Poppy flanked platinum blond Sugar, and the three of them stepped into the club, leaving Eliza outside in the cold.

a spoonful of
sugar makes the
medicine go down

JEREMY HAD PROMISED HE WOULD BE THERE, BUT IT WAS
way after midnight and there was no sign of him anywhere. Eliza
checked her cell phone again, just to make sure she hadn't missed
any of his calls. She walked through the club, checking to see
how many tables she had left in the VIP room. It irritated her to
see Mara ensconced in the best banquette in the house, book-
ended by the Perry twins, holding court with several of the richest young swans of Manhattan society. And it irritated Eliza that
she was irritated. She didn't want to be jealous of Mara, but there
was something just a little off-putting about seeing her friend—
whom Eliza knew couldn't even spell Hermès last year—hanging
out with the teenage heiress to the venerable French couture
house. Mara was hobnobbing with the crème de la crème of the
junior elite, and not only that, she looked like she totally
belonged there.

The girl looked seriously chic. Mara was wearing Sugar's white
Versace dress with a pair of flat-heeled Imitation of Christ gladiator

sandals, and she was holding a slick little art deco cigarette case for a purse. Eliza was wearing her mother's decades-old Alaïa halter dress. The dress was a metallic, thigh-high mock turtleneck with a racer back. It was so tight it hugged Eliza's every curve, and she'd worn it to remind Jeremy what he'd been missing all summer. When she'd gotten dressed that evening, Eliza had felt pretty good about herself, but now she just felt average.

"Hey, cool dress," Sugar said, catching up with Eliza in the coed restroom, a shiny stainless steel room with an industrial trough for a sink.

"Thanks, it's vintage," Eliza said, feeling gratified. Although she hated to admit it, she had missed Sugar's attention. Sugar could be a real bitch when she wanted to—Eliza still remembered how nasty she had been when she'd found out Eliza was working for the Perrys—but she could also turn on the charm when she wanted to. And for some reason, she was doing it now.

"Groovy," Sugar nodded, rinsing her hands. "Congrats, by the way."

"Thanks," Eliza sighed. She was happy she'd won—she could certainly use the money, and she loved being in the spotlight—but it bothered her that it was already one in the morning and Jeremy still hadn't shown up like he'd promised.

"What's wrong, doll?" Sugar asked, powdering her nose out of a T. LeClerc compact.

"Nothing," Eliza shrugged. "I just . . . There was a guy I was supposed to meet here tonight."

"Our old gardener?" Sugar asked, not unkindly.

"Yeah," Eliza nodded, frowning at her reflection in the mirror.

"I thought you were with Ryan," Sugar said.

"Who told you that?" Eliza asked, startled. They'd only hooked up once earlier in the summer, and neither of them was planning to do it again.

Sugar smiled mysteriously. "He *is* my brother, you know. And there was that whole thing with you guys down in PB."

Eliza looked crestfallen. She'd forgotten the twins knew about that. "It's nothing. We're not together."

"Why not?" Sugar asked, leaning against the sink and folding her arms across her chest. "He's not good enough for you?"

"No, it's not that. Of course not."

"Then you guys should just be together," Sugar decided, as if she'd resolved a complicated matter.

"But what about Mara?" Eliza asked anxiously.

Sugar rolled her eyes. "You think Mara doesn't know about you guys?"

"Mara knows?" Eliza asked, a little taken aback. Why hadn't she said anything to Eliza then? Because she was mad? Or because she honestly didn't care anymore?

"It's *so* not a big deal. She's with Garrett now," Sugar declared, pecking Eliza on the cheek. "See ya."

Much later that night, after all the celebrities had departed and Sugar's entourage—including Mara—had left Seventh Circle for a party at Jet East, Eliza saw that she had a message from Jeremy. She went outside to listen to it. Apparently, he'd been stuck at a benefit with his boss that he'd thought he'd be able to get out of. Blah, blah, blah. Eliza heard glasses clinking and girls laughing in the background. He said he was really sorry. Sure he was. Eliza erased the message, too angry and disappointed to care anymore.

She walked inside to the VIP room, where she saw Ryan Perry, who was sitting by himself at a corner table. She sat down next to him, noticing the bouquet of flowers he'd tried to give her earlier. This time, she would remember to accept them.

they shoot models,
don't they?

"WHAT'S SO FUNNY?" MARA ASKED, ARRIVING LATE TO meet Jacqui and Philippe and the kids for lunch at Jeff & Eddy's. She'd spent the morning getting pedicures with Sugar and Poppy, and she felt slightly guilty that she'd ditched work again.

"That woman over there just asked us if we were models," Jacqui explained, rolling her eyes and holding up a thick business card. Mara turned to see Mitzi Goober waving enthusiastically at their table. Mara blew kisses in her direction. "What did Mitzi want?" she asked.

"She wants us to work at this show," Philippe explained, handing Mara an invitation.

Mara read the engraved lettering. It was an invitation to a charity fashion show at the Bridgehampton Polo Club next week. She'd received one the other day in the mail, with a front-row seat designation. Sugar and Poppy had been talking about the event nonstop since then—apparently, it was going to be one of the biggest events of the summer. "You guys should do it," Mara said.

"Modeling is so silly," Jacqui declared, cutting up Cody's string beans.

Mitzi Goober rushed over, air-kissing Mara's cheeks. "So, you guys are all set, right? Reinaldo is going to love you guys. Seriously, it would be such a huge favor, since a couple of the models couldn't get their visas renewed in time."

"So it's a favor? What will you do for me in return?" Philippe asked, smiling wickedly.

"Oooh, you're a bad boy," Mitzi cooed. "I like that. What do I have to do?"

"We'll do it," Jacqui said flatly, cutting in. Did Philippe have to flirt with everybody in sight? Philippe was supposed to be hers—even if all they'd done was sneak a few kisses here and there since the tennis tourney. If agreeing to walk in the show was all it took to get rid of this annoying girl, she was happy to do it. Plus, Eliza and Mara were both going to be there, and Jacqui wished the three of them would get their asses together and be best friends again.

"Fabu!" Mitzi said, blowing air-kisses all around. "See you later, lover. I'll get us a room," she joked, growling at Philippe.

A room, huh?

Now there was an idea.

booty calls totally don't count

IF ANYONE EVER ASKED, ELIZA WOULD TELL THEM SHE WAS totally not in love with Ryan Perry. Not at all. They both had their reasons for wanting to keep their relationship—if that was even a word for what they were doing—quiet.

After Jeremy flaked the night of the tennis tourney and Eliza found out Mara knew—and didn't care—about her and Ryan, it just felt natural to do it again. He'd brought her flowers, for goodness' sake. That night they'd gone back to the Perry estate and, well, the next thing she'd known, they were naked. That was the third time that year. Maybe it was a pattern?

The next morning, Eliza had sneaked out of Ryan's room, taking care not to use the side stairway that led to the back of the house that the au pairs often used. Even though Sugar said Mara knew, she was paranoid about bumping into her. Eliza couldn't totally shake the feeling that fooling around with Ryan was like playing with someone else's toys.

Now, ten days later, Eliza was getting more comfortable with the idea. They'd hooked up a few more times, and it had been fun and casual. The other night, after 50 Cent celebrated his album release at Seventh Circle, Ryan had popped over to the club around closing, and they'd gone back to her place, ostensibly to watch a DVD again, but somehow things had gotten kind of friendly. A couple of days later, he'd called her on her night off and asked if she wanted to come over for *Godfather III*. She hadn't really felt like it (Sofia Coppola might be a great director now but she was a bad actress, Eliza thought), but she'd found herself there anyway. Eliza decided that hooking up with Ryan was like eating standing up in front of the fridge. It didn't count. Zero calories.

Except her parents were being so annoying about the two of them, treating Ryan like her boyfriend, which he was so not. One night, Ryan came over and the two of them microwaved a pizza and hung out by the pool instead of going to a party at the PlayStation2House like they'd planned. Her parents had gotten home early from some charity shindig, and her mom and dad hadn't been able to stop making a big deal out of him being there. Of course, Ryan was an old family friend and all, but still. Her mom winked at the two of them, and then the next morning her dad said Ryan could come over to visit any time he liked, which was interesting, since after Jeremy had come over for dinner, her dad had said maybe it wasn't such a good idea to have people around the house since it wasn't theirs. Eliza supposed that had to do with Ryan being the right sort of person to have around, and Jeremy the wrong sort—according to her parents' logic, anyway.

Not that Jeremy even tried to see her anymore—she'd hardly heard from him since the night of the tournament. Of course, that didn't stop her from checking her messages obsessively.

"Who're you calling?" Ryan asked, shoving a handful of kettle corn in his mouth and spilling crumbs all over the carpet. He'd picked her up from work that night, and now they were just hanging out, watching TV.

"Just checking my messages," Eliza said.

Ryan nodded. On the screen, a popular actress was explaining away her latest disastrous relationship to Oprah during the show's 3 A.M. repeat.

The thing was, it was fun doing whatever it was she was doing with Ryan. It was fun when he picked her up from the club, since everyone knew him or knew of him, and all the waitresses and bartenders thought he was such a doll. It was fun not worrying about anything. Even the guilt over Mara was getting more distant every day. Sugar had said Mara knew and didn't care, so it wasn't like Eliza was doing anything wrong. Being with Ryan reminded her of her old life in New York, when she would kiss any boy she wanted to, just because she could.

"Hey, isn't that Sugar?" Eliza asked, looking up at the screen from her list of text messages. It was the E! reality show. They were covering the tennis match.

Ryan grunted in a disapproving manner. He was about to

change the channel when something caught his eye. Eliza saw it too—Mara, in the corner of the screen, staring longingly at something—or someone. And when the camera panned to where she was looking, there was Ryan, sitting in the stands, intently watching the game.

Huh.

the best things in life are (still) free

"TELL ME THOSE AREN'T REAL!" MEGAN PRACTICALLY
screamed, lunging at Mara's ears as she pulled her hair into a
ponytail. "They're the size of ice cubes!"

The day of the benefit fashion show, Mara had received two
visitors: her sister Megan, toting a huge battered suitcase and a
fifteen-pound bag of makeup, and a brown-uniformed messenger
bearing a small black bag. Inside the bag was a velvet case with a
pair of ten-carat diamond earrings worth two hundred and fifty
thousand dollars, on loan from one of Mitzi's new clients.

Now they were on their way to Jean-Luc East, where Mara
was friendly with the owner. "Yup. Nicole Kidman wore them to
the Oscars," Mara responded. "I'm supposed to wear them
tonight."

After the two were seated at one of the best tables in the
restaurant, Mara's sister filled her in on the latest news from
Sturbridge—trouble on Dad's construction site, Mom's work at
the church rummage sale—but it all sounded so small-town and

hokey to Mara's ears that she found herself spacing out without meaning to.

"And the Infusium sales rep is so cute!" Megan squealed, getting Mara's attention. Every week the salon got a delivery of beauty products, and the Infusium rep—a nice Irish guy named Bobby O'Donnell—was Megan's current crush.

Mara looked at her sister from behind her oversized Chanel frames: Megan was taller than Mara, with red, curly hair and a loopy Julia-Roberts-like grin. She was fearsomely pretty, whip-smart, and in love with a guy who delivered boxes of shampoo and conditioner for a living. What gave?

"You can do a lot better than Bobby O'Donnell," Mara said, cutting short any more discussion on the beauty product sales rep. She'd forgotten how boring life was back home. Had it always been that way?

After lunch, Mara opened her handbag and left a few bills on the table, dismissing Megan's charge card. "I got paid today," she explained, patting a fat brown envelope.

They spent the rest of the day browsing among the East Hampton shops and then returned to the Perry house in time to get ready for the show. Mara looked at herself in the mirror. She was wearing a skinny Christian Dior evening dress with hand-beaded pearls and a feathered hemline. Scott Barnes, the famous makeup artist, and one of Mitzi's clients, had arrived to do her makeup. He'd attached custom fox-fur lashes to hers, just like he did for J.Lo., and Edward Tricomi, who'd given half of

Hollywood their shaggy cuts, had personally cut and styled her hair for the evening. On top of that, she was wearing ten carats' worth of flawless ice on each of her earlobes.

Megan came out of the bathroom. "Isn't this the best?" she said. "I got it from Loehmann's!"

She was wearing a Marc Jacobs mod minidress with big plastic buttons and knee-high white go-go boots. It had been a huge hit . . . *two* seasons ago.

"Why don't you borrow something from me?" Mara asked, motioning to the racks of clothes that were stuffed with the latest fashions. "Really, I don't mind."

"Are you kidding? I bought this especially for tonight!"

Mara groaned. Her outfit practically screamed, "Over," which wasn't exactly what you wanted your fashion show ensemble to say. Mara knew it was wrong, but for the first time, she felt a little embarrassed to be related to her sister.

don't hate them because they're beautiful

BACKSTAGE, THE DESIGNER'S ASSISTANT, WHOSE REAL name was Octavian, but who preferred to be addressed as "Miss O," gathered the models around. "Listen, people!" he yelled. "Boys! Wear your willies down! Girls, you are ski bunnies on vacation! *Hot, hot, hot!* Got it? Okay? Okay!"

Jacqui stood in her first outfit, a skimpy thong–tank top combination and a pair of very low-cut bootleg jeans. The tank top stopped about halfway down the midriff, so that in the back was merely a thin line of fabric that tucked into the jeans' waistband.

She nearly hadn't made it to the show, and now she wasn't all that pleased that she had. When she and Philippe had agreed to model, they had completely overlooked the fact that they would need to be there the whole day. The only thing that had saved them was an overnight retreat for the kabala camp that Anna had insisted the kids attend. She was determined to have the kids befriend Lourdes and Rocco, who were rumored to be in attendance as well.

At the show, Jacqui couldn't believe how stupidly they were being treated. All the production assistants and wardrobe dressers talked to them very slowly, as if they were children, or mentally challenged, or mentally challenged children. Each model had a team of no fewer than three people to herd him or her from makeup to hair to dressing station.

Octavian ran over. "Jacqui! I've been looking for you. Reinaldo has a new vision for the finale." He herded her over to the hair dock, where intrepid stylists were turning the girls' manes into gravity-defying rats' nests, and the lead designer, Reinaldo, was approving each model's updo.

"So, I was thinking," Reinaldo said, touching Jacqui's silky black hair, "what about Sinéad, with a little Good Charlotte thrown in?"

"Divine!" Miss O agreed.

Jacqui sat on the chair, looking quizzically at the two of them.

The hair stylist held a razor in his hand. "Darling, how do you feel about a Mohawk?" he asked.

"You can't be serious!" Jacqui said, reaching up protectively to cover her head. Her long, lustrous black hair!

"It is imperative!" Reinaldo declared, suddenly positive. "Punk-rock wedding, retro meets old-school. Have you seen the movie . . ." he said, frowning and snapping his fingers. "*Star Wars: Attack of the Clones?*"

"More like a fauxhawk, you know, spiky but messy," Octavian nodded. "Richard Avedon meets Helmut Newton in a Baz Luhrmann fantasy!"

skinny-dipping

"Genius!" the hairstylist pronounced.

Before Jacqui could reply, he was shaving into the side of her scalp. It hurt, and a few minutes later, a broom was sweeping up Jacqui's hair, and she was stricken, looking at herself in the mirror.

She'd always taken her looks for granted—but this? She reached up, feeling the downy duck's back that her scalp had become.

"Perfecto! Beautiful!" Octavian gushed.

Jacqui had never felt uglier in her entire life.

that's why they call it b-list, baby

THE BRIDGEHAMPTON POLO CLUB HAD SET UP A HUGE white tent for the fashion show in the middle of the polo field. A line of white tables greeted Mara and Megan at the entrance, and several guests were walking around drinking cocktails, their heels sinking into the grass. Mara spotted Eliza manning the first table and pulled Megan with her to the very front, pushing and murmuring "Excuse mes" while Megan apologized to everyone they jumped in front of. Alan and Kartik had "loaned" Eliza to Mitzi to help run the show, since half of Mitzi's office had had an allergic reaction to a client's new face cream. Apparently, unprocessed seaweed extracts were not for everybody.

"Are you sure this is okay?" Megan asked.

"Excuse me—sorry—excuse us. Sorry, could you move?" Mara asked, stepping forward without waiting for an answer.

Several Waspish socialites cast annoyed glances in their direction, which Mara ignored.

"'Liza!" Mara called.

Eliza, wearing her signature headset and a pretty black-and-white Temperley dress she'd bought with her tournament winnings, waved them over.

"See, I told you—she's a friend of mine," Mara said, not bothering to explain that Eliza had also been one of the au pairs the year before.

Mara pecked the air on either side of Eliza's cheeks, while Eliza did the same to her. Things weren't exactly normal between them, but on the other hand, they weren't exactly estranged, either.

"Eliza, this is my sister Megan," Mara said.

"Oh, hi!" Eliza smiled. "Wow, you guys look so much alike!"

"Really?" Mara asked, not sure if it was a compliment. Hanging around Sugar and Poppy had made her think everyone was always being sarcastic.

"You are gorgeous!" Eliza told Megan, and Mara felt relieved.

Eliza looked down at her clipboard, frowning. "I don't see Megan on here," she whispered to Mara.

"Um, you don't?" Mara asked. She'd meant to ask Mitzi for a seat for her sister, but she'd completely forgotten.

Eliza glanced down. Several of the celebrities they'd been expecting still hadn't shown up, and there was a very slim chance that they would even make it.

"Follow me," Eliza said, pulling back the tent flap. The two Waters girls followed Eliza inside. A long white runway with plastic covering ran the length of the room, and on either side, white folding chairs were arranged in neat rows. Each chair held a small black bag filled with numerous beauty products and glossy magazines, but the bags in the front row were considerably larger than the others.

"Here you go," Eliza said, finding a seat with Mara's name on it. Eliza peeled off the name of a celebrity on the seat next to it. "Megan, you're here too."

"Thank you," Mara mouthed.

Megan plopped down, her eyes agog over the commotion. At the end of the stage, photographers were setting up their tripods and cameras, and a roving band of paparazzi were snapping pictures of the people seated in the front rows. There were famous fashion editors hiding behind their signature sunglasses; a cadre of young, mostly blond women wearing pastel-colored cashmere sweaters around their necks; and a smattering of famous actresses sitting in the best seats. Perky "news" correspondents from all the celebrity news shows and networks—*Access Hollywood, Entertainment Tonight, The Insider,* E!, VH1, the Style Network—were interviewing fashionistas, socialites, and celebrities.

Mara crossed her legs and angled her face for the best shot, knowing that they would soon make their way over to her and take her picture. She was pretending not to notice that her sister was already rooting in the goody bag and exclaiming over the items inside it.

"Look, Mar—free Kiehl's lip balm!" Megan said excitedly, showing her the loot.

Mara nodded, smiling. "It's the best," she agreed. She didn't mention that the company had sent her a carton of its products just the other day. Mara smiled at a tiny, curly-haired woman in enormous sunglasses who was sitting down next to Megan.

"Oh my God! I loved your show!" Megan said turning to look at the woman. "I'm totally a Carrie!"

"Thanks," the star replied modestly.

"Can I get your autograph?" Megan asked.

Mara almost died. Even though Sarah Jessica Parker happily obliged, Mara was embarrassed—celebrities totally didn't come to fashion shows to be hassled by fans. It didn't help that once the photographers had stopped taking Jessica Simpson's picture and started taking Sarah Jessica's, none of them even stopped to take a photo of Mara Waters.

Contrary to what Mara had grown to believe, she wasn't nearly as famous as she thought.

it's getting hot
in where?

JACQUI TRIED NOT TO LOOK INTO THE MIRRORS THAT WERE everywhere backstage. Her hair! Her glorious, beautiful, thick, black hair! Gone! Replaced by some trendy haircut—a fauxhawk, the stylist had called it—a halfway, wussy Mohawk that was long in the middle and gelled to a point, while the sides were short and cropped. She ran her fingers over the rough edges, shuddering at the buzz cut on the nape of her neck. It felt like it belonged on a boy. But there was no more time to think about it, because the lights went down in the front of the house and Octavian was in front, yelling at all the models to get in line.

She tried to find her spot, her eyes bleary with almost-tears—how could she face the world with this ridiculous haircut? She readjusted her bodysuit thing—was it on backward?—pulling it off her shoulders and letting it hang around her waist.

"Jacqui?"

She turned around—completely topless. "Yes?"

"Oh! Hi! Oh!" Kit Ashleigh stood at the perimeter of the

dressing area, his face turning purple. He was holding an enormous bouquet of flowers. "God! I'm so sorry!"

Jacqui folded her arms in front of her chest to cover up. "Kit!"

"I'm sorry I'm late. These are . . . for you," he said, thrusting them at her and averting his eyes.

"They're so beautiful! *Obrigado.*"

A dresser slipped the tank top–thong back over her shoulders, but it didn't really make a difference. Jacqui was still very nude.

Kit did a double take. He'd just noticed her hair. "Your hair!"

"What do you think?" Jacqui said, nervously touching the ends. "Ugly, huh?"

"You look . . ." Kit's eyes shone with admiration. "You look awesome."

"You really think so?" Jacqui smiled, raising her eyebrows in a hopeful expression.

Just then, one of the production assistants spotted Kit. "No boyfriends here!" he said, ushering Kit out of the door.

"I'm not her . . ." Kit blushed again, to the roots of his blond hair. "You look beautiful. Good luck."

"'Bye! Thanks!" she called, as her dresser straightened the thong string into the back of her pants.

Then something bronze and sculpted and perfect caught her eye—Philippe, in the middle of changing, his lean, tennis-toned body naked. He was doing pull-ups on a dressing rack, hanging—*ahem*—out there, for all the world to see, when Jacqui caught his eye.

He shot her a wolfish grin. "Nice haircut!" he called.

There were so many beautiful girls backstage, but for once, he was only looking at her. She ran to her place in line. The lights dimmed outside, and Reinaldo exhorted them to think, *Sex! Sex! Sex!*

After seeing Philippe naked, that wouldn't be too hard.

musical chairs isn't just for kindergarten

A FASHION SHOW WAS THE LAST PLACE ELIZA WOULD HAVE thought to bump into Jeremy, but here he was anyway. She had been helping to keep track of the donation checks, cross-referencing them with the checked-off names on the list, when he appeared at the entrance with Carolyn Flynn. The two of them were huddled together in the second row—sponsor seats, since Morgan Stanley had underwritten most of the event—sipping from champagne flutes and looking around with bemused expressions.

Eliza was watching them, wondering if Carolyn and Jeremy were a couple, when she saw Ryan enter from a side door and slip into his seat beside his sisters. Eliza's heart melted a little bit. So what if Jeremy didn't like her anymore—she had Ryan, and he was a great friend/hookup/whatever-they-were. Ryan winked and gave her a little wave.

Eliza waved back, just as she was accosted by a heavyset woman who looked a little familiar. "Are you in charge here?" the woman demanded. She was wearing a faded black polo shirt and baggy black pants, and was holding a Motorola walkie-talkie.

"Er . . . yes, I suppose," Eliza said. "Can I help you?"

"My client, Chauncey Raven, is about to arrive," the woman said, and Eliza remembered where she'd seen the woman before. She was the pompous publicist who'd asked Eliza not to let Ondine Sylvester into the VIP room earlier in the summer.

"That's wonderful—we love Chauncey," Eliza said, giving her standard reply to the assistants of the famous.

"Well, yes, but I need to know where she's sitting. Those girls over there said all the front-row seats are taken."

"Oh!" Eliza exclaimed. *Shit*. The show was about to start in five minutes. Her headset squawked with Mitzi's grating voice "Eliza! Dollink! Code Blue! Chauncey Raven doesn't have a seat!"

The heavyset handler scowled at Eliza.

Eliza didn't know what to do. Mitzi's command to *fix it!* didn't really translate to anything helpful. How? Bring one seat from the second row up to the front? She scanned the room, which was filling up with guests, and settled on Mara and Megan. Surely they would understand how important it was to have Chauncey in the front row. Eliza click-clacked on her heels down the plastic-covered runway to where they were seated.

"Mar, can I talk to you for a sec?" Eliza asked, pulling on Mara's arm.

"What's going on? Anything wrong?" Mara asked.

"Chauncey Raven is coming to the show."

"Oh, great!" Mara had hung out with Chauncey so much at Seventh Circle, she considered her a friend.

"But there aren't any more front-row seats left. I'm so, *so* sorry. But do you think we could move you and your sister back to the second row? I can put you guys right there, behind the Perry twins."

Mara straightened up. "But why?" she asked, noticing the Perry twins whispering across the runway. Sugar and Poppy were smirking, checking out Megan, and Mara blushed to think of what the twins were saying about her sister's outfit. She couldn't believe Eliza was asking them to move. Mara had been in the Hamptons long enough to know that being asked to give up your seat was completely humiliating.

Chauncey Raven's publicist gripped Eliza's arm and whispered, "Chauncey is in the building! Now!"

"I'm really sorry to have to do this," Eliza said, turning away from Mara and making a begging gesture to Megan. "But we have a really important celebrity attending who forgot to RSVP, and we really need these two front-row seats. I'm totally sorry, Megan."

"No prob!" Megan said, beaming. "Who's the celeb?"

"Really, Meg, you don't have to get up," Mara pressed, even as Eliza was helping Megan out of her seat.

"It's for Chauncey Raven. Thank you, thank you, thank you," Eliza said, handing Megan her things and moving her to the second row. "Oh. Except you have to leave the goody bag."

Megan's face fell. She noted the significantly smaller goody bag on the second-row seat.

"Okay, keep it," Eliza said. "It's fine."

Chauncey arrived a full fifteen minutes later, with husband Daryl Wolf in tow. Since there was only one seat for the two of them, Chauncey promptly sat on her husband's lap.

The room went pitch black, and suddenly, a booming bass line thundered from the overhead speakers, and a sultry British voice began to rap in a sexy coo. The lights went up, and the models strutted on the runway to the beat of the electroshock hip-hop song "Fuck the Pain Away."

The crowd thrilled to the nasty lyrics and the tiny little outfits. Jacqui came out in her tank top–thong and new fauxhawk, and there was an electric shiver in the air. It was all so bad . . . yet so good. Not one outfit was wearable. Not one item of clothing had any reference to the lives of any of the women sitting in the audience. But it didn't matter. The collection was a joyous celebration of sex and youth, and it would garner rave reviews in the papers. By the time the collection hit department stores, the sheer shirts would be lined, the miniskirts cut to a more modest length, and the tank top–thongs—well, they were really only for show.

Eliza put two fingers in her mouth and whistled, looking back to where Mara was sitting. But she didn't see Mara, only Chauncey Raven, who was seated sideways on her husband's lap, completely blocking Mara's view of the runway.

And that's what being a bitch will get you.

blood may be thicker than water, but nothing beats a VIP table

ONCE THE SHOW WAS OVER AND REINALDO HAD TAKEN his bows, there was a stampede toward the reception on the grounds of the country club. Garrett had arrived just as the show ended and given Megan a once-over before completely dismissing her from his attention. Mara gave Megan her goody bag to hold so she could say hello to her friends.

Once the real celebrities had departed and Garrett appeared at her side, the paparazzi finally noticed her. Mara saw that Megan seemed to be feeling awkward, but Mara had to say hello to so many people—gossip columnists, magazine editors, the various publicity handlers whose clients' designs Mara had worn at some point during the summer.

"Dollink!" Mara screeched, saying hello to a slightly over-weight girl in a tight Liberty print. She had finally figured out what Mitzi was saying to her all the time—"darling," in an affected British accent. Not that it had stopped her from copying it. "You look fabulous!" Mara said.

When the girl turned away, however, she whispered to Garrett, Megan, and anyone else who was in earshot, "If you call wearing a tablecloth fabulous!"

Garrett laughed, and the Perry twins sauntered over to join the fun.

"Oh, wow," Sugar said, when she saw Megan's outfit. "I *loved* that dress."

"Really?" Megan asked. "Thanks."

"Yeah, last season," Sugar snickered. "I gave mine away to Goodwill."

Mara pretended not to hear that. She had told Megan to borrow something from her closet, and this was exactly why.

Megan excused herself to check out the buffet, giving Mara a hurt look. Mara shared a cigarette with Sugar.

"God, who can eat at a place like this?" Sugar asked.

Mara shrugged. "Should we go to Dragonbar now?" she asked, referring to the real after-party that only a select few had been invited to, including the three of them.

Several of Sugar and Poppy's friends, including an heiress to a large pharmaceutical fortune, joined their circle. "Hey, Plum, isn't that your sister?" she asked, pointing to Megan, who was having trouble juggling two cocktail-sized plates filled with stuffed mushrooms and crab legs.

"Um, uh, well . . . not exactly," Mara replied, feeling uncomfortable.

Megan didn't hear what she said, but someone else did. Mara looked up to see Ryan Perry staring at her, shaking his head.

"Hi, Ryan," she said, blowing smoke in his face.

"I never would have believed it," he said.

"Excuse me?"

"You've become one of . . . *them*," he said, motioning to the crowd. "My sisters are bad enough, but you . . . I always thought you were different."

"What do you mean by *that*?" Mara asked, but Ryan had already turned and was walking away.

Mara looked around, hoping someone else had heard their conversation and could confirm how totally out of line Ryan was, but there was no one near her, save for a waiter who didn't look exactly pleased to be there. She went back to sit next to Garrett and watched Ryan say hi to Eliza. Megan caught up with her, still holding a plateful of appetizers.

"Mar, I'm exhausted. I think I'm going to go home early," Megan said, looking deflated. "And I think I'll just take the earliest bus back to Sturbridge tomorrow."

Mara was still distracted by Ryan's words "You're just like them." *Like who?* Megan was talking, but Mara wasn't listening. "Um, okay, sure," she nodded, distracted.

"Mara, didn't you hear me? I'm going," Megan said.

But Mara only reached into her purse and handed Megan the keys. "The top lock sticks a bit—you have to turn it twice," she said.

Megan nodded, swallowing. "Well. Okay. I guess I'll see you when you get home at the end of the summer then," she said.

"Yeah," Mara replied, standing up to give her sister an awkward hug good-bye. *Just like them?* Who was *them*—Sugar and Poppy? What was so wrong about that? They were his sisters, after all. Mara looked at them and then back at herself. Sure, they were all wearing metallic sandals and asymmetrical minidresses, but that didn't mean they were the same. *Looks can be deceiving,* Mara said to herself. Ryan should have known that better than anyone.

"Is she gone?" Garrett asked, sidling up to Mara.

"Yeah," Mara said. "She was really tired."

"Good," Garrett said, rubbing her back.

Mara flicked the ashes off her cigarette into an empty wineglass since the ashtray was so far away. Across the room, she spotted Eliza and Ryan huddled in a corner with Ryan's friends. Eliza was sitting right next to Ryan, so that their thighs were pressed tightly against each other's, and Eliza was brushing his bangs out of his face—anyone who saw them would think they were a couple.

See, looks can be deceiving, she repeated to herself again.

Then again, sometimes things are just the way they appear.

i'll break your stupid french face

ELIZA BUMPED INTO KIT, WHO WAS NURSING A DOUBLE scotch, when she arrived at Dragonbar. "Hey, dude, what's wrong?" she asked.

Kit motioned to where Jacqui was huddled in a corner with a crew of glamazons.

Everyone else at the party was dressed like gilded lilies, but the true beauties—Jacqui included—were lounging in sweats and sneakers. Jacqui was sitting squarely on Philippe's lap.

"C'mon, let me buy you another drink," Eliza said. "Maker's Mark, right?"

Kit nodded, shaking the ice cubes in his now empty glass.

Philippe walked up next to them. He nodded to Eliza. "'*Allo*. I think we have met before, yes?" he asked flirtatiously.

"Yes," Eliza nodded, smiling.

Philippe was still wearing makeup, which looked totally goofy up close. He nodded to the bartender and ordered a cosmopolitan.

"Philippe, this is my friend Kit. Kit, this is Philippe. He's one of the au pairs this summer at the Perrys'," Eliza explained.

"Hey," Kit said, watching as Philippe took a big slurp of his girly cocktail. The model in eyeliner was a pink-drink man. "You with that girl?" Kit asked, motioning to Jacqui.

Philippe cocked an eyebrow. "What if I am?" he asked.

"Well, she's a friend of mine," Kit said, trying not to let his voice betray more anger than he was feeling.

"Oh yes?" Philippe raised his eyebrows.

"Yeah. And if you break her heart, I'll break your stupid French face," Kit snarled, poking a finger at Philippe's chest and sloshing the pink drink down his silly MODELS SUCK T-shirt.

"*Merde*," Philippe cursed, turning away without a response, wiping at the pink stain on his T-shirt as he walked away.

"Don't worry about it, baby," Jacqui said, when he sat back down. "We'll get you out of that T-shirt soon enough."

eliza does the relationship math

IT WASN'T THAT HE DIDN'T INTRODUCE HER TO HIS best friend from prep school—Matt Hooper, whom he'd mentioned a couple of times. He certainly did. He'd said, "Hey, Matt, this is Eliza." And Eliza had smiled up at Matt, and Matt had said, "Yo," and taken a seat. That was it. He didn't give her the special once-over or the subtle nod that said, *So, you're my buddy's girl*. Eliza was just Eliza. Just some chick sitting next to Ryan at a club.

They'd been hooking up for more than a month now, and while she didn't expect Ryan to introduce her as his girlfriend . . . she wasn't *not* his girlfriend either. When they'd first gotten together, she'd still thought of Ryan as Mara's boyfriend. But since Mara was so obviously Garrett's new girlfriend, that made Ryan . . . *her* boyfriend? Eliza mentally calculated what Ryan had done for her—picked her up from the club so she wouldn't have to drive, called her every evening, never made plans to see her on the weekend because it was already assumed that he would, of

213

course, see her on the weekend. He'd even given her that necklace before they left Palm Beach. Maybe Eliza was crazy, but it sure sounded like girlfriend status to her.

And if she was his girlfriend, why didn't he say so? Why didn't he tell his friends about her? Why didn't any of them realize that she wasn't merely Ryan's date for the evening, or Ryan's friend, but the girl he went home with every night? Suddenly, Eliza stopped feeling confused, and started feeling incredibly . . . *dissed.*

"Ryan, can I talk to you for a second?" Eliza asked.

"Sure, babe," Ryan nodded, smiling.

"I mean, just the two of us?" she clarified.

Eliza led him to a corner of the club. "What exactly do you think we're doing?"

"Having a drink?" Ryan shrugged, still smiling warmly at her.

"No, I mean . . . the two of us . . . you know."

"Oh." Ryan's face went blank for a second; then he realized that Eliza was looking at him intently. "Well, the way I see it"—Ryan waggled his eyebrows, obviously trying to make light of the situation—"we're like friends . . ."

Uh-huh.

" . . . with benefits. You know . . ." He shrugged his shoulders and tried a winning smile.

"Benefits? What kind of benefits?" Eliza demanded. She knew the term, but she was angry enough to demand that he give her his explanation of it.

"You know . . . we're friends who like . . . hook up and stuff."
Ryan grinned. "C'mon, let me get you another drink."

Where the hell did Ryan Perry get off being so casual about
them? "So that's all I am? A hookup? A booty call?" Eliza spat.

"E, don't be that way," Ryan said, putting his arms around her
to calm her down. "C'mon, it's not what you think. Don't be
mad. You knew what we were doing, right?"

"Fuck you, Ryan!" Eliza blinked back tears. She wasn't cheap,
but that's exactly how she felt like right now.

"Eliza . . . wait . . . Eliza!" Ryan stammered. "C'mon . . ."

Several heads turned in their direction, watching the lovers'
spat that was obvious to all. If any of Ryan's friends *had*
thought Eliza and Ryan were just friends, then the sight of her
throwing her drink in his face made it quite clear that they
were anything but.

love is blind, but maybe mara had sunglasses on

"WHAT WAS *THAT* ALL ABOUT?" MARA ASKED, GESTURING to Ryan, who was following Eliza out of the club. She had watched the whole thing—and although she couldn't hear anything they'd said, it was pretty clear that Eliza and Ryan had been fighting.

Fighting the way only two people who had gotten naked and trembly together could fight.

Sugar sniggered into her drink. "Don't you know?" She licked the side of her martini glass and smiled at Mara innocently.

Poppy elbowed her sister.

"Eliza and Ryan hooked up in Palm Beach. I've heard they've been hooking up all summer. He's at her house, like, all the time," Sugar told Mara, in a matter-of-fact voice.

Eliza . . . and Ryan? Together? Her best friend! And her boyfriend! Okay, her ex-boyfriend! And fine, her ex–best friend! But . . . Ryan! And Eliza! In Palm Beach! Together! And all summer, too! How could she have not known?

How could Eliza not understand the first commandment of friendship: *Thou shalt not hook up with your friend's crush, boyfriend, or ex-boyfriend.* Or the second commandment: *Thou shalt not lie to your best friend.* But Eliza had spent all of last summer skulking around the Hamptons, lying to all her old friends about moving to Buffalo and being an au pair. Maybe she'd had been wrong about Eliza all along.

"Sweetie—we thought you knew," Sugar said, with a light hand on Mara's shoulder.

"Are you okay?" Poppy asked, looking concerned. She handed Mara a cocktail napkin. "You're not crying, are you?"

Mara shook her head and forced herself to smile. "I'm all right, really."

But really, she wasn't.

jacqui is the victim of nokia interruptus

A MOTEL KEY.

That was what Jacqui slipped into Philippe's jeans pocket at Dragonbar when he wasn't looking. "I got us a room," she explained when he found it. "It's in Montauk, not far from the beach."

Screw Anna and her ultimatums. Philippe was worth the risk.

The motel was an old ramshackle fifties-style beach resort, with clean rooms and wall-to-wall carpeting. It wasn't the Bentley, but it wasn't something out of *Psycho*, either. Jacqui disappeared into the bathroom. They were finally together—alone, in private, and away from the eyes of Anna Perry. She looked at herself in the bathroom mirror, still not used to seeing her hair so short, and slipped into the Agent Provocateur ensemble she'd bought especially for this occasion.

Philippe was lying in bed, under the covers, already naked when she came out of the bathroom. He grinned when he saw her. "Ah, the Agent Provocateur," he said knowingly.

Hmm. Not quite the reaction Jacqui had expected. She believed a real compliment was, "You look beautiful in that dress," not, "Your dress is Chanel," but maybe Philippe was just super fashion-savvy because he was French.

She pulled the blankets aside and slid in beside him.

"Ooof! Your feet are freezing," Philippe complained when she snuggled next to his body.

"Sorry!" she said, rubbing her ankles on the sheets. "The tiles were cold in there."

Philippe calmed down and began to kiss her. She closed her eyes, feeling his hands move across her body, pulling at the delicate bows holding her lingerie together. Philippe suddenly propped himself up on his elbow and looked around the room.

"What?" Jacqui asked.

"My phone," he said, jumping out of bed and running to the corner, where his backpack was buzzing. He kneeled down and unzipped the front pocket, where his phone was lit up and vibrating.

Jacqui fell back into the bed, sighing loudly, but Philippe was already talking into his Nokia. "No, no, I'm not doing anything," he was saying. He hung up and looked at Jacqui. "I'm sorry. . . . I have an, uh, emergency," he said.

Jacqui watched, speechless, as Philippe put his clothes back on. When he ran to the bathroom to wash his face, she lunged for his backpack. Who the hell could be so important that he'd leave her—*naked*—in the middle of the night? She scrolled feverishly down the menu. The last received call: *Perry House.*

Anna.

Of course.

that's why they call it
the walk of shame

WAKING UP IN AN UNFAMILIAR BED IS NEVER FUN.
The way the sunlight hits you—lemony-stark, unflattering, and
speckled with dust—it's like the world is punishing you for your clan-
destine actions the night before. Even though Mara hadn't hooked up
with Garrett the night before—he'd passed out fully clothed the
minute they'd gotten into bed—she woke up feeling wretched. Ryan
and Eliza were together, and the thought made her chest clench.

Garrett was still sleeping when she got up to put on her
clothes from last night. It felt gross—cheap—to wear a feathered
evening gown in the morning, and she'd slept with all her
makeup on. She looked for her Blahnik sandals but couldn't find
them anywhere.

"Heymmmppf," Garrett said, opening one eye and trying to
pull Mara back into bed. "Whereareyougoing?"

"I've got to go," Mara said, feeling frantic as she removed his
arms from her waist. She picked up her purse from the carpet
and scurried out the door without her shoes.

"Illcalllurrggh," Garrett mumbled.

She sped out the side stairs through the servants' entrance, and through the back yard that separated the Reynolds and Perry properties.

She'd just cleared the hedges in front of the pool, when Ryan appeared with a surfboard tucked under his arm. Just *great*. Just the guy she wanted to see.

Ryan took in Mara's wrinkled dress from the night before, her bare feet, her smeared makeup, and the direction from which she'd come. His face registered contempt.

"Late night?" he asked with an angry smirk.

Mara squared her shoulders. Nothing had happened, but she wasn't going to tell him that. Let him think she'd spent the night with Garrett—let him think she didn't care about him one bit.

"Garrett kept me up for hours," she said, smiling as widely as she could force herself. "I'm *sooo* tired."

Ryan's face contorted angrily. He looked disgusted with her.

"I know about you and Eliza," she said. "So don't even think you're so much better than me."

"What are you *talking* about? You broke up with me in November!" he yelled.

It was the first time Mara had ever seen Ryan show any real anger, any indication that his laid-back, anything-goes attitude could be rattled. It was exactly what she'd needed to see last fall when she'd told him they should just be friends.

"Only because I didn't think you really . . . Oh, forget it,"

Mara said, turning away. It was too late anyway—he was with Eliza now. She turned and walked briskly back to the au pairs' cottage, trying not to think about what had just happened.

When she got to their room, it was empty. Jacqui was nowhere to be found, and Megan was gone. She hadn't even left a note. Mara collapsed on the single bed, mentally, physically, and emotionally exhausted. The intercom rang.

She picked it up. "Hello?"

"Is that any way to answer the phone?" Anna Perry's clipped voice asked.

"Oh, sorry," Mara answered.

"The children are waiting for their breakfast. Am I correct in assuming you still work for us?"

"I'll be there right away, Anna," she said grudgingly, wondering where on earth Jacqui had disappeared to, and why the fuck she hadn't told her about Eliza and Ryan.

Some friends those two had turned out to be.

babies cry when you take away their candy

KARTIK HAD ASKED ELIZA TO HELP MITZI WITH THE
day-after wrap-up from the fashion show, so now she was back
after only a few hours of sleep. The ground crew was stacking
all the chairs, and empty goody bags blew through the tent like
tumbleweeds. Eliza sat in a meeting with Mitzi and the other
assistants, everyone yawning behind dark sunglasses and sipping
from venti nonfat lattes, rehashing the gossip from the night
before.

"Okay, so we need to messenger a goody bag to any
celeb who didn't get one last night," Mitzi said, looking over
her checklist. "Chauncey Raven's publicist called. Chauncey
needs one."

Eliza nodded. That was *so* like a celebrity. She could have forty
million in the bank, but she really *needed* that Kiehl's lip balm
and Swarovski-crystal-encrusted Sidekick.

"We need to follow up on a couple of items today, too—we
lent several girls a few dresses to wear, and we need to get them

back. Just send the usual messengers. We do have a special case, however. Sugar Perry has a Chanel, and we need to get it back for Karl's show in Paris tomorrow. It's really important, since it's the only sample we have right now. Eliza, you know Sugar, right? Can you handle that personally?"

"Sure," Eliza said, trying not to roll her eyes.

Pulling into the Perrys' driveway, she was glad to see that Ryan's car wasn't there. Last night, Ryan had called her cell phone six times, but she hadn't picked up, and she'd deleted his messages without listening to them.

After throwing her drink at Ryan last night, she'd run out of the club in tears, and right into Jeremy and Carolyn. He'd tried to grab her arm, but she'd kept walking. It was funny how things worked out: All she'd wanted was to be with Jeremy this summer, and now here he was with someone else, and here she was, crying over a guy who wasn't even him. Except that on the ride home, the woods dark on either side of the car as she sped through night, she'd stopped crying about Ryan and started crying about Jeremy.

Eliza rang the doorbell and asked the butler for Sugar. She braced herself for a fight. Sugar Perry wasn't the kind of girl who would give up a one-of-a-kind couture dress that easily.

Sure enough, when Eliza walked into Sugar's all-white bedroom, the first thing Sugar said was, "Who let you in?" She was wearing a sheer T-shirt and boy-shorts, and the reality-TV cameramen were taping her every move.

Eliza shrugged. "Mitzi wants the dress back."

"What dress?" Sugar asked innocently, doing back-bends. Sugar had been up since dawn, doing sun salutations. She always got up early, regardless of a hangover.

"The Chanel. It's the only one, and we need it for Karl's show."

"Oh, that one," Sugar said. "I don't know where it is."

"You lost it?" Eliza asked, incredulous. "I mean, you wore it home, didn't you?"

"I suppose." Sugar giggled. "I don't remember."

"Listen, Sugar, I really don't care. I'm just doing my job. Could we get the dress back? It's not yours, you know."

"Fine," Sugar said. She opened the door to her dressing room and rooted in the pile of clothes on the floor. She tossed a shredded silk rag at Eliza.

"Oh my God," Eliza said. "It's ruined."

"Charlie stepped on the train, and I think Poppy burned a hole in it with her cigarette. Sorry!" Sugar smiled fakely.

Eliza held up the pale pink Chanel dress to the camera. She couldn't believe anyone could be so reckless, even someone as spoiled as Sugar Perry. "You know Daria Werbowy is supposed to wear it on the runway tomorrow! Mitzi told you to be careful!" Eliza spat at her.

"I was careful. It wasn't my fault, okay?" Sugar said impatiently. "Besides, can't he just, like, make another dress? I mean, that's what designers do, right?"

Eliza stuffed the dress into a brown paper bag, pushing past the cameramen. Eliza knew Mitzi would be furious, and that she, rather than Sugar, would bear the brunt of her fury. Celebrity trumped all else. That much Eliza had learned this summer.

the best things in life
are . . . covered by
insurance? (let's hope!)

WHEN MARA ARRIVED BACK FROM HER DAY OF BABYSITTING, she was still seething that Jacqui hadn't told her about Eliza and Ryan. She'd hardly seen Eliza all summer, but she'd slept in the same room as Jacqui almost every night.

"Ivan Jewelers called for you," Laurie said, as Mara shooed the kids into their playroom.

"Oh?"

"They sent a messenger this afternoon to pick up some . . . earrings? But you hadn't left a package or anything, so I sent them away."

The earrings. The two-hundred-and-fifty-thousand-dollar earrings. Right. Mitzi had told her they would send someone to pick them up the day after the party. She'd completely forgotten.

Mara ran out to the au pairs' cottage. The message light next to the answering machine was blinking.

"Mara, hiii! It's Mitzi. You were gorgeous last night, dollink! Anyway, hon, I gotta get those earrings back to Ivan. Put them in the case and just leave them with your assistant so the messenger can pick them up. Thanks! Bye-*yeee*."

"Mara, hiiii! It's Mitzi again. Listen, hon, the messenger says there wasn't a package for him at the house. You must have forgotten. Call me and let me know—Ivan really needs them because J.Lo is going to wear them to the MTV Music Video Awards. Thanks, sweetie. Bye-yeee."

Mara ransacked her dresser. She *swore* she'd taken them off when she got back to the cottage that morning and put them in the little velvet case next to Jacqui's watch, but when she opened the case, they weren't there. They weren't in her other jewelry box, either, or on the sink, where she sometimes put the Mikimoto pearls. Could she have left them at Garrett's the night before?

She called Garrett and explained the situation. "Nope, nothing here. The only thing missing from this room is you, dollface," Garrett drawled.

She hung up on him, frantic.

Could Megan have taken them? No way, Megan had left before Mara arrived home—and please, her sister? She was so honest she'd actually called Target to tell them they hadn't charged her for something she'd ordered. Could she have lost them at the fashion show? Earrings didn't just fall out, did they?

She was certain she had taken them off right when she arrived that morning—right after seeing Ryan—but why weren't they there?

The phone rang. Mara picked it up. "Hello?"

"Mara! Dollink! So glad I caught you. Listen, can you leave those earrings in a package for pickup tomorrow? Thanks, doll!"

"Sure," Mara said weakly, her stomach churning. She'd signed for them so blithely, agreeing to legal and financial responsibility for the value of the earrings in case of loss or theft. But this must happen all the time, right? Mara remembered reading something about Paris Hilton losing a diamond bracelet at some club.

But then, Paris was famous, and as Mara had come to see at the fashion show, she . . . *wasn't*.

with friends like these, who needs the perry twins?

JACQUI RETURNED FROM MONTAUK MUCH LATER IN THE afternoon, since Philippe had taken the car last night without any thought as to how Jacqui was going to get home herself. She'd had to take the bus, which took a winding route and stopped roughly every five seconds. The many hours she spent in transit gave Jacqui ample time to feel incredibly stupid about risking everything just to be with Philippe, especially when he had been Anna's boy toy all along. She was angry at herself for not sticking to her resolution and disappointed that she'd believed Philippe when he'd said there was nothing going on between him and Anna. But they hadn't been caught—not really, anyway—and even if Anna had Philippe, at least everything else was still going to work out, especially the job in New York.

When she got back, she found the au pairs' room in chaos and Mara in the middle of the mess, looking frantic, her hair awry; the sheets, pillows, and blankets piled haphazardly on the perimeter; and all of Jacqui's clothes, shoes, scarves, bikinis, underwear, tissues, and magazines laid out on the bed.

"*Merda!* What on earth? Mara, what are you doing!?"

"You!" Mara accused, looking up from her search. She forgot the earrings for a moment. There was something more important she wanted to confront Jacqui about. "You knew all along, didn't you?"

"Me? What? What are you talking about?" Jacqui said, confused.

"Ryan and Eliza. You were there in Palm Beach. You knew they'd hooked up. And you never told me?"

"Hang on. Hang on," Jacqui said, stepping slowly into the room as if Mara were a cornered and dangerous animal.

"You knew, didn't you?" Mara demanded, her eyes flashing with anger.

"About Ryan and Eliza? Yes, I did. Mara, I'm so sorry. I wanted to tell you . . . I just didn't think it was my business—"

Mara recoiled. "I would have told you if it was your boyfriend!"

Jacqui blinked. "Mara, he *wasn't* your boyfriend. You broke up with him, remember?"

Mara didn't have an answer to that. Instead, she made a throaty noise and resumed her search.

"But what is going on here?" Jacqui asked, taking another careful step into the room, holding up her hands like Mara might attack at any second. "Why is the place all torn up?"

"I am looking—for—my—earrings!" Mara said in an agonized voice.

"O . . . kay . . ." Jacqui said, still holding up her hands. "What earrings?"

"The ones Ivan the Jeweler lent me. The ones I wore last night. Nicole Kidman wore them at the Oscars. They're worth two hundred and fifty thousand dollars. And they need them back, like, tomorrow."

"The ones you were wearing last night?" Jacqui asked slowly.

"Yes." Mara nodded impatiently. Was Jacqui hard of hearing?

"They cost that much?"

"Yes."

"Shit," Jacqui said, beginning to sort through the pile on the bed and help Mara look for them.

"They're not lost. I had them on this morning. I took them off—and put them—there," Mara said, motioning to the dresser. "And now they're gone. Did you see them?"

"No. I mean . . ." Jacqui stammered, rooting through a pile of underwear. *How could Mara be so careless?* "I don't know. . . . I wasn't looking. . . . I just got here."

"Strange, you always seem to know where everything else is," Mara snipped, looking pointedly at the Pucci scarf Jacqui was wearing in her hair.

"What are you saying?"

"I'm saying that it's incredibly strange, isn't it? They were here when I left—but they're not here when I got back. And you seem to feel fine helping yourself to the rest of my things, so—"

"Are you suggesting that I took them?" Jacqui asked, not quite sure if she'd understood Mara's English correctly.

233

"I'm just saying they're not here. And you're the only one who has the key to this room aside from me."

Jacqui had never been so insulted in her life. She stared at Mara, who suddenly seemed like a stranger to her.

"Maybe *you* took them," Jacqui said coldly, wanting to say the meanest thing she could think of to Mara.

"Why would I?" Mara asked, alarmed.

Jacqui shrugged. She put down the stack of clothes she was sorting through. She wasn't about to help Mara do anything.

Just then, the door opened, and Eliza entered, not realizing she was walking into a landmine.

"Oh, look! Another lying slut," Mara said. She'd had enough time to get really worked up about Eliza and Ryan while she'd been desperately searching. "You probably took the earrings just to spite me or something."

"What are you talking about?" Eliza asked, confused.

Jacqui quickly explained about the earrings.

"Listen, Eliza, I know you've been jealous of me this whole summer. I know you just want what I have, but I really didn't think . . . I didn't think you would do something so underhanded."

"What are you *talking* about?" Eliza demanded, leaning forward as if that would help her understand why Mara was being such a total bitch.

Mara snapped. "I know all about Palm Beach."

Eliza looked startled. "But I thought you already knew about Palm Beach. I thought you didn't care."

"Who told you that?" Mara scoffed.

"Sugar," Eliza said.

"It doesn't even matter if I knew or not," Mara spat. "I can't believe you would do something like that to me."

"You guys had broken up! And I did mean to tell you . . . but then Sugar and Poppy said you already knew and didn't care . . . and . . ." Eliza said, her voice trailing off when she realized what a mistake she had made. Of course Sugar had lied to her. That was what Sugar did—she lied.

"So you think it's okay to date my boyfriend behind my back?"

"Your *ex*-boyfriend. You have a *new* boyfriend now, Mara. Or did you forget? And we weren't going behind anyone's back. We just didn't want anyone getting hurt," Eliza said.

We. We. We. That hurt Mara more than anything Eliza had said. She and Ryan were a *We.* The two of them, Ryan and Eliza, were a couple.

"But you knew how I felt about Ryan," Mara said. She could have lived with knowing they'd had a one-night stand in Palm Beach, maybe, but a whole summer of the two of them? Together? Behind her back? What was Eliza thinking? "You knew I still liked him," Mara said.

"How would I know that? We barely hung out this summer," Eliza argued.

"Yeah, you ignored me the whole time," Mara replied.

It was true. Eliza had avoided Mara out of guilt at first, but as the summer wore on, and her job wore her down, and Jeremy ignored her, she had found comfort in Ryan. She'd been using Ryan as a Band-Aid to forget about Jeremy. But the Jeremy wound had never healed. She was still in love with Jeremy, and she'd wasted the whole summer with Ryan. And lost a best friend.

Mara, Eliza, and Jacqui stared at each other, hating one another for more reasons than they could possibly say.

it takes e-v-i-l to spell *handsome devil*

MARA HAD TURNED THE ENTIRE COTTAGE INSIDE OUT, searched the footpaths and the bushes next to the pool, the country club grounds where she'd brought the kids that day—although the possibility of both earrings falling off her ears was highly unlikely. As the days passed, it was looking more and more like someone had deliberately stolen them.

Mitzi Goober had taken to tele-stalking Mara—her cell phone, the phone in the room, and the main house phone rang incessantly, and it was always Mitzi or one of Mitzi's assistants asking if Mara could please call back and let them know when Ivan could expect his earrings returned. Mitzi had even come by herself, since the MTV Awards show was in two days, but thankfully Mara had been out with the kids at the beach. Finally, Ivan himself had called, screaming and threatening legal action.

It was a Thursday evening, and Garrett was supposed to pick her up at seven so they could go to a dinner his parents were throwing at Alison by The Beach to celebrate the sale of his movie—*Casablanca in Space*—to a studio. But seven came and went, and the Maybach failed to appear in the driveway. Seven-fifteen, seven-thirty. Eight o'clock. The dinner was supposed to start right now.

Mara looked at her watch. She dialed Garrett's number again, but there was no answer. She felt sort of ridiculous just standing around in her Roland Mouret kimono dress and peep-toe Prada heels, waiting for him to arrive. Finally, she drove herself in the BMW to the party. Maybe she was supposed to meet him there?

The restaurant was airy and light, with a copper bar and all-white bunting hanging from the ceiling. The Reynoldses had rented out the whole restaurant, and Mara noticed several people staring at her strangely as she looked around the room for Garrett.

"Hey, do you know where Garrett is?" Mara asked a girl who was dating one of Garrett's friends.

"He's over there," the girl said. "But, um . . ."

Mara ignored her and walked over to the main table in the middle of the room, where Garrett was sitting with his chair tipped back, laughing uproariously. She walked up to him and rubbed her hand down his arm.

"Er, hi. Sorry I'm late," she whispered, looking for an empty seat at the table. There wasn't one.

Garrett turned around, obviously surprised to see her. "Mara, what are you doing here?"

"I was waiting for you. I thought you were going to pick me up," Mara said, wondering why he was looking at her like that.

He'd told her about the dinner last week and had made her promise she'd be there.

"Excuse us one second," Garrett said, leading Mara away from the table. She noticed a tall, exotic-looking girl glaring at them.

"Wait a minute—are you here with someone else?" Mara asked.

"You didn't get my message?" he whispered urgently, leading her farther away from the crowd.

"What message?" Mara asked, stepping aside so a waiter could deliver a tray of champagne glasses to a nearby table.

He sighed loudly and ran his fingers through his bangs. "I uh . . . I'm really sorry, Mara. You're a great girl and all, but you know, no hard feelings."

"Excuse me?" she asked, noticing that everyone at the party was settling into their seats and several people were shooting Garrett concerned looks.

"Listen," he said, looking like a guy whose patience was being tested, "I can't be seen with someone like you right now. My dad is getting all this bad press about our house, and if he finds out the girl I'm dating . . ." He trailed off.

"What?" Mara asked.

"Oh, Mara. Everyone knows you took the earrings." Garrett smiled. "I think it's awesome, actually. Great job sticking it to Mitzi. You know her firm doesn't have liability insurance, right? Her career is over." He chuckled.

"But I didn't take the earrings. *I didn't,*" Mara said. "And I can't believe you would think that of me."

"Listen, babe. It doesn't matter what I think. I told you, I don't care if you did take them, but I can't have any bad publicity right now. My dad is going to go ballistic if my name is attached to yours any more this summer. It was bad enough when people chatted about your . . . you know . . . background. But this is worse."

Mara shook her head. She didn't understand what Garrett was saying. What background? What press? What bad publicity? How did he even *know* about the earrings? Then Mara remembered: This was the Hamptons. Everyone knew everything.

"So you're dumping me?" Mara asked.

"Mara, you're a nice girl, and we had some good times, right?" Garrett said, winking at her. "It was worth it for the Perry factor alone."

Perry factor? Mara opened her mouth to ask what the hell he meant by that, but Garrett was already back at his table, raising his glass in a toast.

To himself, natch.

seventh circle of hell, indeed

"YOU SEE THAT TABLE OVER THERE?"

Eliza nodded. She looked over to where Kartik was pointing. It wasn't just a table, it was *the* table—the table that Mara had danced on the night of the nipple photo, and the one that Chauncey Raven usually commanded.

"Make sure they get extra-special treatment," Kartik said.

Eliza nodded and walked over to the table to deliver her standard welcome: a monologue on the services offered at the club, with a personal gesture—a bottle of the most expensive champagne. It was a pretty little speech that never failed to impress the VIPs, who, if male, would drool over Eliza, wondering if she was part of the "services provided," or, if female, would try to bond with Eliza, since most celebrities had been waitresses or hostesses until they hit it big.

"Hi, I'm Eliza. I just want to welcome you to Seventh Circle," Eliza said, beginning her speech, when she noticed who it was that had caused Kartik to single the table out. "Sheridan Dunlop?"

"Oh my God. Eliza!"

Sheridan Dunlop had been a year ahead of Eliza at Spence but had dropped out and moved to Los Angeles after her junior year. She'd since cornered the market on icy blond Wasp princess roles, now that Gwyneth Paltrow had joined the ranks of stay-at-home moms, and had recently been nominated for an Academy Award for her portrayal of a deaf-mute prostitute. She was sitting with a bunch of old friends from New York and the Hamptons. Carolyn Flynn was there, as well as her old friends Taylor and Lindsay, and . . . *Jeremy*?

"Hey, Eliza," Jeremy said casually, as he smoothly took the bottle of champagne from her grasp. He was actually sitting between Taylor and Lindsay, and Lindsay had her hand on his knee.

Eliza was stunned. She'd thought all along that Jeremy was with Carolyn, but now it was even worse. Lindsay—Lindsay, that smug little copycat wannabe with the bad nose job and the hyena laugh. She was looking at Eliza like she'd won a prize.

"Hi, Jeremy. Great to see you, Sheridan," Eliza said, walking away.

She was holding back tears on the back patio, shakily smoking a cigarette when Jeremy found her.

"'Liza," he said, touching her shoulder.

"They're just using you, you know," she said quickly. "They're the kind of people who . . . who . . . they don't even really like you. They just want something from you. Lindsay's not exactly an honest person, you know."

Jeremy raised his eyebrow, pulling his lips into his mouth. "You know, I'm not sure you're exactly in a position to be talking about *honesty*. I know all about you and Ryan Perry."

Oh.

there's more than one kind of pond scum

THE NEXT MORNING, MARA WAS SUPPOSED TO HAVE a massage at Naturopathica with Poppy and Sugar. She was looking forward to it, since the stress of the lost earrings was definitely getting to her.

"Have you seen the twins?" Mara asked, bumping into Laurie outside their bedrooms.

"I think they left."

"They did? How?" The twins hadn't had their own car for weeks.

"I think they took Poppy's BMW," Laurie explained.

That was *her* BMW, but Mara didn't feel like correcting Laurie, who'd been pretty cold ever since Mitzi Goober had mistaken her for Mara's assistant at the beginning of the summer.

Still annoyed, Mara walked into the kitchen and flipped through the newspapers. *GEORGICA POND DRAINED OVERNIGHT!* blared the latest issue of the *East Hampton Star*. Georgica Pond was a pretty lagoon and nature preserve next to the ocean, where she and Ryan used to walk and the kids liked to play. It was also home to the piping plover, an endangered bird. Someone had dug a ditch through the fifty-foot beachhead to drain the pond water into the ocean overnight. There were "before" and "after" pictures, and Mara didn't even recognize the swampy mess in the "after" photo.

Ezra Reynolds was named as the prime suspect because he had publicly complained that the pond overflow was disturbing his construction, and he had been denied a permit to legally drain the pond. The article mentioned that those who lived on Georgica Pond "frequently saw themselves as above the law," and that neighbors included Calvin Klein, Martha Stewart, Stephen Spielberg, and Ron Perelman, who had all issued stern denials. The Reynolds contingent was suspiciously mum on the matter.

Mara felt more than a little repulsed. What kind of person—what kind of family—would be so selfish? Those poor little piping plovers. She picked up the *New York Post*, immediately turning to Page Six to read their gossipy take on the Pond Drain Mystery. But a different article caught her eye: *QUARTER-MIL MISHAP!* Mara sat down, swallowing as she read.

Which not-so-wellborn girl who dated one It Boy last year and traded up for an even richer boyfriend this summer was loaned a pair of million-dollar earrings for an event and hasn't bothered to return them?

It was a classic Page Six blind item, except that it went on . . . and on.

"She said she misplaced them, but I think they're stolen," an *anonymous source revealed. "I thought she was a friend of the Perry twins, but she's from some cow town or something." Sugar Perry, when asked for a quote, said only, "So many people claim to be my friend, and I've never met them in my life!"*

"Totally," her newly brunette sister Poppy added.

The article did everything but name Mara, although her identity wouldn't be too difficult to figure out from the incriminating details.

"I didn't steal them!" Mara said to the empty kitchen, her face ashen. So that was why the twins hadn't waited for her this morning. They had already written her off. The *Daily News* had a story about the earring scandal as well, and another gossip columnist lambasted her as a greedy, stealing au pair.

Garrett and the twins' brush-off would only be the first of many, she knew. Mara had never felt so deflated and rejected in her life.

It was raining hard when Jacqui returned from her SAT class late that night to find a shadowy figure on the lawn, holding an umbrella and combing the grass with a flashlight. Poor Mara. Even if Jacqui was still mad at her, it still made her sad to watch Mara searching the grass in the middle of a downpour. A flash of lightning lit up the sky, and Jacqui realized the figure was too tall to be Mara.

It was Ryan.

"Hey," Jacqui said, calling to him. "What are you doing?"

"Oh, hi, Jacqui," Ryan said, pointing his flashlight in her direction. "I lost my, uh, contact lens and I was looking for it."

"I didn't know you wore contacts," Jacqui said.

Ryan shrugged, and Jacqui smiled sadly.

If only Mara knew how much Ryan Perry still loved her.

the piping plovers have never been so popular

ALLAN WHITMAN AND KARTIK COULDN'T RESIST A CHANCE for publicity, and the weekend after the pond scandal, they quickly put together a benefit party for the homeless plovers at Seventh Circle.

Eliza found Jacqui in the middle of the crowd and hugged her. It was the first time that summer Jacqui had set foot in Seventh Circle, and she was impressed with the way Eliza controlled the crowd and worked the room. Neither of them mentioned how hurt they were by Mara, but they both knew what the other was thinking.

Eliza saw Ryan come in and walked over to his side. They hadn't seen each other in a week, and in that time, she had stopped being angry about the friends-with-benefits thing and had started wanting to be actual friends again.

"Hey," she said, bumping an arm on his shoulder.

Ryan managed a smile. "Hey, yourself."

She kissed him on the cheek, brushing the corner of his lips by accident. "I'm sorry about the other night," she said.

"I'm sorry too," Ryan said. "I didn't realize . . . I mean, I want to say, I really do care about you, Eliza. And I don't know what I was saying. I mean . . . you know you're more than a friend to me. We can be a couple if that's what you want."

"I know," Eliza said.

Ryan held out his arms and Eliza stepped into them. She nestled her head on his shoulder and he tightened his arm around her waist. It should have been enough, but it wasn't. Because just then, across the room, she spotted Jeremy and Lindsay walking into the VIP room.

Jeremy had slicked his dark hair back and was wearing a brown cashmere sport jacket and dark denim jeans. Lindsay had her arm snaked around him in a vise grip and was looking up at him adoringly. He bent down to whisper something in her ear, and Lindsay laughed as if she'd never heard anything funnier in her life. Eliza's heart clenched.

Ryan went to get them drinks, and Eliza turned to look out the window. It was still raining hard outside, like it had yesterday, but that didn't stop people from waiting outside the club as usual. Then she saw Mara at the door, underneath an umbrella, being turned away by one of Mitzi Goober's minions.

Eliza saw Mitzi Goober pretend not to see Mara. Mara was one of the few people who actually cared about the plovers, and Eliza knew it had taken courage for her to even show her face to this crowd. J.Lo had attended the MTV Music Awards wearing Harry Winston, and Mara had been blacklisted.

Mitzi's assistants asked Mara to step aside, and, against Eliza's better judgment, her heart went out to her. Mara slowly turned away, but not before peering through the plate glass window and seeing Ryan kiss Eliza on the forehead and hand her a drink.

It's not what you think, Eliza thought. But even if Eliza had wanted to run out of the club to call her name, Mara was already walking away.

something's about to blow

THE NEXT MORNING, JACQUI AND MARA WOKE UP TO the sound of an explosive crack.

"*Merda!*" Jacqui said, throwing off the covers and looking out the window.

"What's going on?" Mara asked.

It had been raining for several days now, but nothing like this. The wind howled and raged against the windowpanes, and the two of them had gotten dressed in silence, since Jacqui still wasn't talking to Mara. They ran into the main house, where Laurie had already turned on the television to the news channel. Hurricane Tiffany was coming in from North Carolina, but instead of moving over land and weakening, as had been predicted, it was moving over water and picking up speed.

"It's going to hit tonight," Laurie said grimly. "We're going to have to get the house ready. Where are the kids?"

Philippe helped Laurie find the storm windows in the basement and started hammering them on the sills.

A quick reconnaissance of the pantry revealed a lack of fresh water and other supplies, so Laurie called Ryan on his cell phone and told him to go to the nearest Home Depot and stock up on bottled water, flashlights, batteries, candles, towels, canned goods, and other sundries.

Zoë ran up to Mara. "I'm scared," she said.

"It's going to be all right, sweetie," Mara said, hugging the little girl. "Just let me go a minute."

Even as the rest of Long Island was battening down for a major hurricane, the relentless business of publicity marched on. Now that Mara had been knocked off her pedestal and was rumored to have been dumped by Garrett Reynolds, all the designers wanted their clothes back. Pronto. Which meant Mara spent half the day tracking down flashlights and towels and the other half running back to her room and handing back all the shopping bags to the messengers. It was all so humbling and shameful, especially when one of Mitzi's assistants had arrived to tally up the total, just to make sure everything was there and accounted for.

"This Chloé blouse hasn't been cleaned," the assistant said rudely, checking it off of a list. "Okay, so we're just missing the Sally Hershberger jeans, the rhinestone Blahniks, and the Pucci scarf." She sighed.

"I don't, um, have them," Mara stammered, hating the way it sounded coming out of her mouth, especially after the earring scandal. The brown-uniformed man from the delivery company gave her a sympathetic look.

"Fine, I'll just tell Mitzi you stole those, too," the assistant said snidely as she opened her umbrella and stepped outside.

Jacqui couldn't help but notice the parade out of the cottage. She held an armful of four-by-fours to help reinforce the front door and nodded to Mara as Mara led the assistant to the garage to pick up the BMW.

Poppy drove up in the car, and when she and Sugar heard that Mitzi had asked for it back, their matching faces contorted into a grimace. "What do you mean she wants it baaa*aack*?" Sugar whined at the publicist before giving back the keys. "We're the ones using it now!"

"You really are an idiot, Plum," Poppy complained, as they stood in the open garage, watching the BMW disappear down the driveway.

You have no idea, Mara thought.

eliza is an over-it girl

AT NOON THE SKY WAS PITCH BLACK, AND THE STREETS were deserted. Everyone had battened down the hatches to prepare for the worst storm of the year. Eliza stood on the deck of her rented house, in a yellow parka with the Spence crest on its front pocket, watching for Ryan in the Cayenne. Her family had asked her to get supplies, and Ryan had offered to pick her up.

Ryan threw open the passenger door. He too was wearing a yellow windbreaker with his school crest, jeans, and his usual flip-flops. He told her it was a mess back at the house—none of the flashlights were working, and they were short several storm windows. Plus the water had begun to trickle in the front door, and they were already out of towels.

"I know, you'd think the people who own our rental would have stuff, but they just have all this dinky crap," Eliza said.

"Anna is having a nervous breakdown. She can't live without her hair-dryer if the power goes out."

Eliza giggled at that and, catching Ryan's eye, they both chuckled again.

They drove slowly through the rain, and it seemed that every car on the highway was going their same direction. When they arrived, the parking lot at Home Depot was completely filled. Ryan managed to snag a spot just as a Bentley pulled out, a generator strapped to its roof.

The rain was coming down in huge droplets against the windowpane. The trees were bent backward by the wind. The storm howled and raged, shaking the SUV.

"God, look at that," Ryan said, as the wind carried a beach umbrella through the parking lot.

"I know. It's crazy." Eliza nodded. "And you know what else is crazy?" she asked quietly.

"What?" he asked, clearly having no idea what she was about to say.

"You and me."

Ryan's smile faded. "What do you mean?"

Eliza looked at Ryan. His hair was pasted to his forehead, but he looked as gorgeous as ever. But in the end, they were just too comfortable around each other. Too similar. Eliza craved mystery, spontaneity, the kind of guy who would get a job as a valet at a party just to be close to her. As wonderful as Ryan was, he wasn't that guy.

"You're not in love with me," Eliza said.

Ryan began to protest.

"And I'm not in love with you, either," she interrupted.

"Ouch," he joked, clutching his heart in faux pain.

"This summer—this summer was like, kind of weird, you know? I thought it was going to be the best time ever." Eliza sank a little deeper into her seat. "I had this cool job—but it turned out to be totally worthless. I'd rather babysit kids than babysit celebrities. Believe me, even William is easier. Ever tried taking champagne away from a celebrity?" Eliza laughed.

"Eliza?"

"Yeah?" She turned to look at him.

"You're the coolest girl I know." Ryan leaned over and cupped her chin in his hands, then lowered her face so that his lips touched her forehead. "Friends?"

"Of course." Eliza laughed. "Stop it, that tickles."

They loved each other—as friends—and Eliza suddenly wanted to see her friend happy. She looked at Ryan again. He was tall, gorgeous, smart, rich, and her childhood friend—the kind of guy her parents always wanted her to end up with—but she knew they weren't meant to be together.

Ryan hugged her, and as she pressed her cheek against his, she whispered, "I know you love me, but I also know you're in love with someone else."

He released her slowly and sighed. "I have no idea what you're talking about." He picked at a cuticle.

"The girl we both love, the girl you're in love with—she's still there," Eliza insisted. "Believe me, I've been pissed at her too, but she's still in there."

He shrugged. "Mara's different now. She's let the Hamptons get into her head. She's changed."

"Look, nobody who goes through the It Girl treatment comes out alive on the other side, you know? Believe me, I know. There's not a girl in the world who wouldn't get carried away. But I still believe in her. I haven't told her that, because we're kind of mad at each other right now. But I think the reason she broke up with you is because she didn't think . . . well, she thinks she doesn't deserve you." It all came out in a rush, and Eliza didn't dare look Ryan in the eye. She glanced at him now, but his face was still stony.

"She's with Garrett now," Ryan said flatly. In that one sentence, Eliza knew that what she'd said was true. Ryan was definitely still in love with Mara.

Eliza looked at Ryan. She was closer to him now than she'd ever been. Maybe the term *friends with benefits* had a deeper meaning than either of them had realized.

"Well, we better go in before it gets any worse," Ryan said.

"And by the way, Mara and Garrett broke up," Eliza said. "I'm surprised your sisters didn't say anything. Aren't they totally hot for him?"

"Eliza, I don't even know how we're from the same family," Ryan joked.

They ran into the Home Depot—but all the steel braces, wood reinforcements, tarps, hurricane lamps, candles, batteries, space heaters, generators, rope, nails, and sandbags were gone.

"What's going on?" Eliza demanded of a nearby foreman wearing an orange vest.

The foreman shrugged. "We got a big order," he said, waving toward a guy leaning against the counter and signing a huge credit card receipt. Garrett Reynolds looked up and waved at Ryan and Eliza.

oscar wilde said, "true friends stab you in the front"

POPPY WAS STILL SEETHING ABOUT THE LOSS OF "HER" car as she and Mara ran into the house to escape the battering winds.

"That is just so rude, I have never been treated so rudely. Do they know who I am?" Poppy whined as she struggled with her umbrella.

Mara was squeezing the water out of her wet hair when something bright and sparkly caught her eye. Something Poppy was wearing on her ears: Huge, fat rocks. Diamonds so big they pulled down on Poppy's earlobes and so clear and perfect they glittered in dull of the entryway.

"Poppy," Mara said, reaching out toward the earrings. "Where did you get those?"

Poppy's hands immediately fluttered to her ears. "Oh, these? Uh . . . I . . . borrowed them from your dresser. I lent you my handbag and I figured, you know, what's mine is yours and what's yours is mine." She giggled shrilly. "Why?" She was totally acting like she and Sugar hadn't completely blown Mara off for the last couple of days, never mind that they had actually talked to Page Six about Mara and the earrings.

"Those aren't mine," Mara said, dumbfounded.

"They're not?" Poppy fluttered her wet eyelashes innocently.

"They belong to Ivan. They're worth a quarter of a million dollars. Haven't you read Page Six? You were quoted in it. People think I stole them."

Poppy feigned innocence. "I have no idea what you're talking about. C'mon, let's go dry off. I'm freezing."

"Wait a second. I need them back," Mara said flatly, holding her hand out.

"Okay! Don't be such a wench about it. *Jeez*," Poppy said, pulling them out of her ears and brusquely laying them in Mara's hand.

Mara just stared at her. She had never met anyone so relentlessly self-centered, so aggressively selfish, in her entire life. And this was the kind of person she'd spent the whole summer trying to impress. It was sickening how much time she'd wasted.

"Now, Plum, don't be mad. I was just borrowing them!" Poppy said defensively.

"Don't call me that!" Mara hissed, elbowing her aside and heading for the phone.

When the messenger picked up the earrings, Mara felt so relieved and deliriously happy, she had no idea what to do with herself. She felt liberated and free, and as she waved away the brown truck, she bumped into Jacqui, who was getting ready to run a few errands before the hurricane really hit.

"Jac! Oh God, Jac!" Mara said, rushing toward her and picking Jacqui's arms up and twirling her around.

"What? What happened?" They hadn't talked in more than a week, and she hadn't seen Mara smile in that entire time.

"Jacqui! I'm so stupid. I'm so awful. I'm so sorry. Poppy—it was Poppy who took the earrings. I don't know if they knew, I don't know if it was deliberate. I think it was, but I'm so sorry I thought . . . you had . . . I must be insane. . . ."

Jacqui raised an eyebrow. The Perry twins. Of course. The twins' bedrooms were the first place they should have looked for the earrings. "It's okay," she told Mara.

"I just want you to know that I'm really, really, really, really sorry," Mara said. "Really, really, really—"

"Mara, look, I forgive you, all right?" Jacqui interrupted, taking her hand.

"It's just, I feel so embarrassed. I wish it had never happened."

"Listen, things happen for a reason. Don't worry about it," Jacqui said as she hugged Mara tightly. "But your apologies aren't over, *chica.*"

Jacqui was right. They were just beginning.

there's nothing sexier than a guy with a hammer

JUST AS RYAN AND ELIZA WERE ABOUT TO LEAVE THE Home Depot empty-handed and disillusioned, a friendly voice called over. "You guys looking to get some supplies?" Jeremy asked. He'd also been stymied by the Reynoldses' great buyout. He walked over wearing a slick vinyl poncho and a crushed fisherman's hat.

"They're all out," Eliza said.

"Yeah, but I know where we can get some," he said. "There's a Target in Riverhead, and they sell storm windows and everything there. Not many people in the Hamptons know about it, since it's in the North Fork. You guys want to follow me? Take the highway north to the Riverhead exit and it's right there." He wiped his hands on his jeans, which were tucked into big rubber fishing boots.

Eliza nodded her thanks, and she and Ryan followed Jeremy as he drove down the flooded highway. There weren't as many cars going in that direction, and they made good time.

Inside the Target, it was as if the hurricane wasn't even happening. It was bright and cheerful, and all the shelves were stocked high with everything they needed. There were several other people shopping, but there was plenty to go around, and they all just smiled conspiratorially at one another.

"Who's going to put up your windows?" Jeremy asked Eliza as they both took some lanterns and heating oil.

"My dad," Eliza said, even though her dad was like, seventy years old.

"I'll do it," Jeremy said quietly. "Look, man, I'll just drive Eliza home," Jeremy said, turning to Ryan. "Her house is on the way to mine, anyway."

"Okay with you, E?" Ryan asked.

"That's fine, actually," Eliza said, her heart beating fast.

Ryan gave Eliza a quick hug. "Good luck. Stay dry!" he said to both of them.

Eliza climbed into Jeremy's pickup truck. The seats were battered leather, and it was nothing like the Porsche Cayenne's sleek leather upholstery or heads-up dashboard display—but it smelled like the earth, piney and loamy, like Jeremy. She loved that smell.

They drove in silence back to Eliza's Westhampton rental, where her parents were frantic with worry. Without a staff to command, the Thompsons had no idea what to do. The television had already gone out and the lights were off, but Jeremy soon found the circuit breaker in the basement and flipped the right switch.

"Oh thank God," Eliza's mother said, tugging at the pearls around her neck anxiously.

"I don't know how long we'll have the juice, but we might as well use it while we have it," Jeremy said. "Power'll probably go out soon."

Eliza watched as Jeremy expertly put up all the windows, hammering and pushing and figuring out the complicated instructions. She hoped her parents could see what she saw in him.

He was working on the attic bedroom windows when she brought him a bottle of water. "It's not cold, I'm sorry."

"No, this is good, thanks," he said, wiping the sweat from his brow. He leaned against the bracing and put his body into it. The joint snapped right into the window, and he smiled in satisfaction. "There, that should do it. You guys have enough towels, right? And a radio?"

"We have a little battery-powered Sony Watchman—my dad found it in the basement. So I think we'll be okay," Eliza said.

Jeremy nodded. "That's good." He sat down on the floor and gulped down the water.

"What happened to you this summer?" Eliza asked, sitting next to him on the carpet.

"What happened to *me*? What happened to *you*?" Jeremy said, peeling the label of the water off.

"I don't know—you like, pushed me away. I didn't think you wanted me anymore," she said. "You never called. You didn't even want to see me."

"Eliza, the only reason I took that internship at Morgan Stanley was so I could be someone you could respect. Someone from your . . . *world*," Jeremy said, making quotation marks with his fingers when he said "world."

"You did that for me?"

"I did, but it turned out I still wasn't good enough. Your parents made that pretty clear at dinner. I figured, I'd never change their minds about me, so why should I even bother?" He shrugged.

"Why *bother*?" Eliza said, incredulous. "Because I don't think like my parents do, that's why. And that's pretty shitty to judge someone based on their family," she said. "People can't help where they come from."

Jeremy looked embarrassed, but then he said, "Yeah, but then I heard about you and Ryan, so . . ." He trailed off.

It was Eliza's turn to looked embarrassed.

"I missed you," she said matter-of-factly.

"I missed you too," he agreed. "I saw you on TV last night," he offered, unexpectedly lightly.

"You did? Where?" Eliza asked, surprised.

"On Sugar's show. You were asking for a dress back and she wouldn't give it to you." He chuckled. "And at the end some old French designer guy in big black glasses was saying that he would never dress Sugar Perry again. It was pretty funny."

"*Karl Lagerfeld?*" Eliza asked, but Jeremy just shrugged. Maybe Sugar would get her comeuppance after all. Eliza looked at Jeremy. Even talking about some stupid TV show, he was still ten times more soulful than anyone else she'd ever met. She'd missed him so much.

"It's just . . . you were always so busy," she said, tentatively pulling at the bottom of his pant leg.

"Yeah, no kidding. I hated that job. Anyway, I quit. You can't believe the amount of bullshit you need to put up with. I'm working at the Perrys' again next summer."

"You are?"

"Yeah, I just told them I'd be back." He finished the last of the water and put down the empty plastic bottle.

Eliza was still processing all this new information. "I thought you didn't like me anymore," she said.

"Eliza, what are you talking about? I'm crazy about you," he said. "I've been crazy about you since the first time I saw you at the Perrys' pool."

"What about Carolyn? Or Lindsay? Why were you with them?"

"I met them through work. Carolyn is cool. And she was friends with your friends. I thought . . . I don't know, I thought that would matter to you, that I knew people you did. Lindsay was nothing. I was only with her because I thought I could make you jealous, since you were with Ryan."

"Ryan and I aren't . . . aren't anything special. We're just friends."

"Really?" he asked hopefully.

"Really," she said firmly.

"So . . . you're not with him?"

"No." But Eliza had to come clean. "I mean, not anymore. He's great, but he's . . . he's just not you."

Jeremy smiled his crooked smile. Eliza smiled into his eyes, and just like that, they kissed. Jeremy stroked her hair, and Eliza put a hand up to his cheek, warming her hands on his skin while the hurricane swirled around them and the house shook.

"I love you," he said. "You're the only girl for me."

Eliza felt so much happiness that she wasn't sure it could fit inside her skin. And when he kissed her again, she felt as light as air, like a bubble that had popped out of a bottle of champagne, floating dizzily toward the ceiling.

mara steals from the rich to give to the, uh, rich

THE LIGHTS WENT OUT AT FIVE, AND THERE WERE NO MORE towels to stop the water from entering through the cracks in the doorway. The kids were getting antsy. Mara had spent the afternoon with them, playing Go Fish and Old Maid. William was actually sitting still for once. Zoë had a knack for Go Fish, and even Cody was being quiet. Madison had even found a bag of chips and was eating them along with everyone else.

"Old Maid!" Madison crowed, when Mara took the wrong card.

"Well, let's just hope it's not prophetic," Mara joked.

The house shook with a rumble that came from the driveway, and they all ran to the window to see an immense Home Depot truck pull up to the front of the Reynolds estate.

Mara couldn't believe it. Ryan had called to tell Laurie that there was nothing at the Home Depot. Looking at the truck, she could only guess what had happened.

"C'mon, kids!' she said, getting all of them together. "We're going to do a raid!"

268

After making sure all the kids were dressed warmly in sweaters and nylon slickers, she led them outside. The rain was coming down hard, and it was going to get really bad really soon. She ushered them through the hedges that separated the property and into a secret passageway that Garrett had showed her, which led to the basement of the Reynolds Castle.

The kids were beside themselves with delight. Mara led them up through the basement. She cracked open the door to the kitchen. The coast was clear.

"C'mon," she said, and led the kids to one of the upstairs bathrooms where the linen closet held so many towels it was like a miniature Bed, Bath & Beyond. Mara began loading up on towels, passing them out to the kids to hold.

"What are you doing?" Garrett asked lightly, walking into the bathroom, holding a beer. He looked pasty in his white oxford shirt.

Mara looked at him. She remembered his cutting remarks, the way he'd immediately believed she had taken the earrings and dumped her without even bothering to listen to her side.

"You guys have too much of this stuff. You don't need all of it, so we're taking some," Mara replied, as if it were the most natural thing in the world.

"You can't do that," he said, still in a light, mocking tone.

"Okay, then I'll ask nicely. Can we have some? Please?"

"No," he replied sharply. "Now please leave and take the brats with you, or I'll have to call security."

"Sorry, Garrett, but that's not going to work," Mara said. "William?"

"Uh-huh?" The little boy asked.

"You know that move they taught you in kickboxing class?" she asked, bending down to his level. "That would come in handy right about now, don't you think?"

Once William realized what Mara was asking him to do, an evil grin spread across his face.

"*Hiii-ya!!*" he said, running straight for Garrett and kicking him—hard—in the stomach, making the older boy double over. "Go, go, go!" William yelled.

Before leaving, Mara spied another something sparkly that had been missing. Her Blahnik sandals. She picked them up from behind the bathroom door triumphantly. Mitzi had already written them off, so they were hers to keep.

"'Bye, Garrett!" Mara laughed.

As they ran out the door, supplies in hand, an older couple who lived up the hill were getting out of their car. They noticed the supplies Mara and the kids were carrying.

"Where did you get that? They're all out of supplies at Home Depot!"

"Here, have some—there's much more!" Mara said gaily, passing over a couple of paper bags filled with batteries and bottled water.

They ran back into the Perry house, flushed with success and triumphant over their loot.

"We found water!" Mara said, marching victoriously into the kitchen and depositing two one-gallon bottles on the table. "Oh." Her face fell.

On the kitchen counter was a huge stack of water bottles, towels, batteries, and firewood. There were candles and heating oil and hurricane lamps and several loaves of bread, canned tuna and baked beans, and towels and rope and flashlights, all in cheerful white plastic bags with the Target logo. The kids began to cheer, tearing into the Cheetos and Pringles.

Ryan stood in the middle of the kitchen, putting away the dried pasta. "Eliza and I found a Target that was open," he explained, without looking at her.

"Oh . . . oh, great." She was about to back out the door, when he called her.

"Wait, I want to—we need to talk," Ryan said. He turned around, and for the first time, Mara could see just how upset he was.

knight in yellow
rain slicker

"*MERDA!*" JACQUI CURSED AS SHE TURNED THE IGNITION and the engine of the little gas-electric hybrid sputtered to life, then went dead. Everyone in the Perry household had taken the Prius's fifty miles per gallon for granted, and Jacqui couldn't remember anyone filling up the tank all summer. Now it was empty, and she was screwed. She was stuck out on Route 27, and the storm was only getting worse.

She tried the Perry house, but the line just kept ringing, which meant the phone lines were probably down. She tried Eliza's cell, but it went straight to voice mail. Even though she was still angry with Philippe, she didn't know who else to call. She hated having to depend on him, especially since he'd never even explained about the other evening at the motel and acted like nothing had ever happened when he bumped into her at the house.

She dialed his cell phone.

"Hello? Hello, Philippe? Listen, it's Jacqui, I really need you right now."

"Hello? Who is this?" a female voice demanded.

"Um, it's Jacqui?" Jacqui replied. What was going on? Why wasn't Philippe answering his phone?

"Well, *this* is an unpleasant surprise," the dulcet tones of Anna Perry said. "I'm sorry to say that Philippe is no longer open for business."

Click.

What? Her hands shook as she turned off her phone. Anna Perry? Then it hit Jacqui: She'd been caught—or at least Anna thought she'd caught her. It was almost comical. After a summer of stealing kisses with Philippe, she'd been caught *after* they'd already stopped seeing each other.

Jacqui sighed, realizing what this meant: She could kiss that job in New York good-bye. No more working for the Perrys over the school year, no more Stuyvesant, no more college. She had risked everything, just for some guy. Some guy who wasn't even worth it. Some guy who was obviously having an affair with their employer. Her whole future—down the drain.

She looked out the window, frightened as lightning lit up the sky. She dialed another number, hoping against hope that the person she called would pick up the phone.

Fifteen minutes, passed, thirty, then almost an hour—the car was being rocked back and forth by the wind. She had to get out of there, or the car was liable to be carried away by a flash flood soon.

Finally, just as she'd given up hope, the headlights of a hulking

Lincoln Navigator appeared out of the fog. A boy wearing a yellow slicker ran to the side of the Toyota.

"You all right in there?" Kit called from under underneath the hood of his windbreaker.

She nodded. He helped her out of the car. The water was ankle deep as they waded through to the behemoth SUV. Kit secured Jacqui's door and ran around to the driver's seat. He grinned at her when he climbed back inside.

"Thank you so much," Jacqui said. "I'm so sorry to bother you."

"Not a bother at all." Kit smiled.

Jacqui returned his smile, and for the first time felt butterflies in her stomach. Maybe it was simply her relief at finally being rescued, but Jacqui couldn't stop smiling as Kit navigated his way through the flooded roads.

He explained that all the roads back to East Hampton were blocked, and they were better off going back to his parents' place in Wainscott. They arrived at the Ashleigh compound, the only lit-up house on the street. While the acreage surrounding the property was enormous, the house itself was just a tidy modern box—a long, squat concrete terminal with floor-to-ceiling windows looking out into the ocean. Kit explained that his dad's best friend was a famous architect and had designed it. Apparently, it was small enough—just two thousand square feet—that the European generator they'd installed could power the whole house for weeks.

Kit drove the car into the adjoining garage and led Jacqui into the house through the kitchen, where his mother was cooking dinner on the Viking stove in an open loft-style kitchen. Unlike the Perry house, the Ashleigh house was a real home—someplace where people *lived*, not just a showcase.

There was a huge black canvas on the wall that could only be a very expensive piece of art, and a few spare wool couches and leather-and-chrome chairs, but there was a newspaper disassembled on the coffee table, and dog hair on the couch, and mugs of coffee on the side tables. The shelves were lined with books, and only a few framed platinum records in an unobtrusive nook hinted at Kit's father's prominence in the music industry.

"Hi, dear. Oh, is that your friend?" Kit's mother asked pleasantly. "Awful out there, isn't it? You must be freezing. Christopher, darling, why don't you give Jacqui a sweater and pants from my closet so she can change?"

There was none of the frantic confusion or unorganized panic of the Perry home, and no towels under the doorways, either. The house was built like a bunker—it was an oasis of art and light and great Italian food.

Jacqui thanked her, feeling undeserving of so much hospitality. After showering in the steam bath and changing into a bulky black sweater and a pair of sweatpants, she had dinner with Kit's parents, regaling them with stories of Brazil and her observations of the Hamptons, and after the Ashleighs retired for the evening, she helped Kit load the dishwasher and clean up the kitchen.

They brought out Kit's duvet and snuggled underneath it on

the couch, watching the news. There were several mudslides reported in the cliffs, and the ocean was rising at a dangerous speed.

"I hope the Perrys are all right," Jacqui said, gnawing on her fingernails. She was worried about them, but also worried about what would happen when she returned. Anna was sure to fire her ass as soon as she set foot back on the estate.

"I'm sure they're fine," Kit said. "I talked to Ryan, and it sounds like they have it under control."

Jacqui leaned her head affectionately on Kit's shoulder. She'd never thought of Kit as anything but a friend, but as she sat beside him on his couch, feeling safe and protected and secure in his warm stone house, Jacqui felt the first stirrings of something deeper—something more than lust—and it dawned on her that maybe this was what really *liking* someone, as opposed to *wanting* them, felt like.

"You've got to give me time," she whispered, putting a hand on Kit's red cheek. He was so pale, his skin was too sensitive, and his hair was so blond it was almost white. He definitely had potential.

"Huh?" Kit asked sleepily.

"Nothing," Jacqui said.

"Are you comfortable?" Kit asked.

Jacqui nodded. She'd never felt more at home.

a bathrobe never looked so good

MARA FELT BAD FOR RYAN. HE LOOKED SO SAD, JUST standing there, dripping wet in the kitchen, a pack of Rice-A-Roni in his hand.

"Listen, you don't have to say anything," she said. The thought broke her heart, but if Ryan and Eliza were happy together, then she would just have to find a way to be happy for them.

"I don't?" he asked, confused.

"I know you and Eliza are together now, and it's . . . fine. I just want you guys to be happy . . ." she said, her voice trailing.

Ryan shuffled and put down the cardboard box. "But that's what I'm telling you—I'm not with Eliza. Eliza and I . . . we're just friends," he said, stepping toward her. "We're good friends, but that's all."

"You're not? With Eliza? But . . . I don't understand," Mara said, taking a step closer to him. Then she saw that his lips were a little purple. "Oh God, you're freezing," she said, before Ryan could say anything else.

"But I want to tell you something," Ryan said, dripping fat, wet rain droplets on the floor.

"Okay, but you need to get out of those wet clothes first," she said, "Come on."

"I *am* c-cold," he said, shivering. "Come with me?" he said as he began stripping off his outer clothes on the way to his room. When they arrived at the top of the stairs, Mara saw that a maid had already started a fire in the fireplace next to his bed. Ryan stood next to it and started looking a little less blue.

"Here," she said, holding a fluffy white towel from the bathroom. "You need to get dry, or you'll catch the flu or something."

"Mara, wait—we need to talk," Ryan said, rubbing the towel against his neck. His T-shirt was drenched. "Do you mind?" he asked, tugging at the shirt.

"Um, oh, no," Mara said, turning around. "Go ahead, I won't look."

Ryan laughed. "No, I mean, will you help me?"

Mara lost all her self-consciousness as she helped him out of his soaked clothes. He stripped off his wet jeans, and Mara handed him his bathrobe. He looked so handsome, so tan against the terry cloth, so nearly naked. . . .

"So, Mara . . . I just wanted to tell you . . ." he said awkwardly. "I mean, this is kind of hard to say."

"Yes?" Mara looked at him hopefully.

"It's just that, well, this summer, you know, I . . . just . . . I just . . ." He shook his head and looked grimly into the flames.

"I missed you this summer, you know," he finally said. He exhaled. "I guess I missed—I *miss*—the old Mara."

"I do too," Mara said, her throat tightening as she sat down on the side of his bed, deflated. The old Mara. The Mara before the earring scandal, the Garrett Reynolds debacle, the Perry sisters' nickname. She didn't know who the old Mara was anymore. She certainly wasn't just some small-town girl from Sturbridge anymore, but she wasn't a Hamptons swan, either.

"Ryan, I feel awful. I've been terrible. I just . . . I just . . ." Her eyes filled with tears, and when they fell, she couldn't stop them. "I just got carried away, and all I wanted was to be with you. I don't even know why I was with Garrett all the time. I just wanted to make you jealous."

"Well, it worked." He laughed, sitting down next to her.

"I kind of think he was only with me to make you jealous too," Mara said. "When he broke up with me, he said it'd all been worth it for 'the Perry factor,' whatever that meant."

Ryan shook his head. "He's been like that since we were kids. He stole my first girlfriend, back in sixth grade. Sophomore year, I took this girl to the winter ball and he took her home." He shrugged. "He's a douche."

Mara squeezed his knee sympathetically and smiled at Ryan's summation of Garrett's personality. He *was* a douche.

"You know, I really lost it when you broke up with me," Ryan said. "I should have said something, I should have come down to Sturbridge. Tried to get you to change your mind . . ."

"I just never thought a guy like you could be my boyfriend," she admitted. "I thought if I broke up with you first, I could make it easier on myself."

They hadn't been looking at each other when they were talking, preferring to confess to the fire, but finally, Mara turned to face Ryan. She pushed his bangs off his forehead.

"I did so many things this summer that I regret," she sighed. "I've been so awful to Eliza and Jacqui. And I was so rude to my sister when she was here."

"Eliza and Jacqui and your sister will all forgive you," he said reassuringly. "It's all going to be all right."

"No, everyone hates—" But before she could finish, he was kissing her. And she was kissing him back. It was so sweet it was almost painful.

He pulled her toward him, his fingers lost in her hair, and she wrapped her arms around him. They kept kissing and kissing and kissing, without stopping to breathe, as if the only thing that mattered was pouring their souls into each other through their kisses. She shivered, and he pulled his bathrobe open, wrapping it around her, too.

Mara closed her eyes, elated and anxious. There was no one else for her, and no one else for him. He was everything she'd ever wanted, and even though she was still anxious that she'd made a mess of a million things, she let her body melt into his. It was as if they were made for each other, and their bodies were telling each other what their hearts had been feeling for a long, long time.

so that's why william was so out of control

THE NEXT MORNING, THE FLOOD HAD RECEDED AND sanitation workers were beginning to clear the highways of fallen trees and branches. Kit drove Jacqui back to the Perry house, the Navigator plowing through the deep, muddy waters. The winds had died down, and it had finally stopped raining. The storm had moved north, but the Hamptons were devastated. Several homes on cliffside bluffs were completely destroyed, and as Kit pulled up to the Perrys' driveway, they noticed that the Reynolds Castle—what was left of it, anyway—had taken a severe beating.

"Yikes," Kit said, his eyes dancing. "I hope they had insurance."

"It was such an eyesore, it's a blessing," Jacqui said.

She felt more nervous looking at the Perry house. It was almost time to face the music, and she was *so* fired. But as she was gathering her resolve, getting ready to pack up her things and head unceremoniously back to Brazil, a junky old taxi pulled into the other side of the circular driveway. Philippe opened the trunk and stacked his suitcases inside.

He was leaving? Jacqui hadn't realized he wasn't staying for the whole summer, but then again, she hadn't realized a lot of things about him. She looked at the beautiful boy and felt stupid, but not heartbroken. Philippe gave her a mild wave.

"Where are you going?" she asked.

He shrugged and put on his sunglasses. "*Au revoir, ma cherie.*" He shook a cigarette out of his pack before climbing into the back of the taxi.

Laurie came barging out of the house. "And don't come back! You're lucky we're not pressing charges! If it weren't for your aunt, you'd be in a lot of trouble, young man!"

Dr. Abraham pushed past Laurie, carrying his battered plaid suitcases. "Hold on, boy! I need a ride to the train as well!" Dr. Abraham gave Laurie a sheepish nod and followed Philippe into the car.

Jacqui walked up the waterlogged steps. The Perry house seemed to have survived intact. "What happened?" she asked Anna, who was watching everything from the foyer.

The frosted blonde looked Jacqui up and down. "Don't you know?" she asked suspiciously.

"Know what?" Jacqui asked, mystified.

"But you called Philippe last night . . ." Anna said.

Jacqui blushed. "I . . . I was stuck out on Route 27. The Prius ran out of gas and I was trapped outside in the hurricane.

I tried the main house, but the lines were down," she explained.

Anna's face visibly relaxed upon hearing Jacqui's explanation. "So you really didn't know?" she asked again.

"Know *what*?"

"Philippe is a drug dealer," Laurie interjected, breathlessly recounting how Anna had found out that Philippe and Dr. Abraham were selling Ritalin, Adderrall, Valium, and Ambien to customers in the greater Hamptons area.

So *that* was why his cell was always ringing. Apparently, Philippe had started nicking William's prescriptions to fill some orders, and when the doctor had found out what Philippe was doing, instead of reporting it, he'd supplied Philippe with more scrips and gotten a cut of the deal. The hurricane had made a lot of people nervous, and Philippe had made a lot of deliveries that week. Anna had discovered the truth when she'd caught him stuffing William's pills in his backpack, when she'd been running around the house looking for *her* meds. And *that* was why Anna had said, "Philippe isn't open for business," when Jacqui had called.

Anna didn't want a scandal and had chosen to send Philippe away and fire the doctor rather than take any legal action. She found the whole thing more unseemly than criminal. She didn't want her name in the papers. At least, not for this sort of reason.

Anna dismissed Laurie and then touched Jacqui's arm conspiratorially. "By the way, congratulations on keeping away from him all summer." Anna winked. "I know how charming he can be."

Even though Jacqui hadn't entirely stayed away from Philippe, she didn't think there was any reason to mention that now. Maybe Philippe hadn't been with Anna—the emergency call from the Perry house the night at the motel could have just as likely have been Dr. Abraham. Jacqui would probably never know for sure, but she also didn't care.

"Anyway, Jacqui darling, I just wanted to remind you that we'll need you to be back in New York by late August. I'll send a ticket to your address in Brazil—will that be all right?" Anna asked.

"Does that mean I get the job?" Jacqui practically squealed.

"Of course." Anna nodded. "And my friend at Stuyvesant said we'd be able to get you in, no problem. We're not sending William to Eton after all, since he failed the entrance test. And after everything that's happened with Philippe, I don't think his aunt—our usual nanny—will be coming back. So we're definitely going to need someone to help with the kids."

Jacqui laughed. After all that, she was getting everything she'd wanted. And, looking at Kit, who was helping Ryan clear the wreckage of fallen limbs, she realized that maybe she had ended up with even more than she deserved.

summer ends early,
but the next one
isn't too far behind

THAT AFTERNOON, ANNA ANNOUNCED THAT THE
Perrys were going to go back to New York early. There were a
couple of weeks left before Labor Day, but staying around to
clean up the house and yard was not Anna's idea of a good time.
The girls were still going to get paid for the whole summer as had
been agreed, but after that evening, their services would no
longer be required.

Since the kitchen was unusable due to water damage, Jacqui
proposed a full-blown Brazilian *churrascaria*—grilled steaks,
sausages, chicken, and lamb, to celebrate surviving the hurricane.
Now that the storm had passed, the sky was bright and clear and
the air was warm. It was the perfect night for a barbecue. Jacqui
even made a pitcher of caipirinhas, a Brazilian version of the
mojito, that she knew her friends would like.

She invited Eliza to come over and join the fun, and although
Eliza was a little hesitant at first, she agreed. She had a lot to say
to Mara, and it was finally time. She and Jeremy arrived at dusk,

his trusty old pickup truck carefully maneuvering over the bumpy roads and around the fallen trees. They walked over to the patio, where the smell of sizzling meat wafted deliciously in the air. The kids were running around, sword fighting with the fallen branches.

Eliza saw Mara and Jacqui manning the grill. Mara was fresh-faced and glowing. For the first time that summer, she was wearing her own clothes—a plain white T-shirt and a pair of Gap cargos.

"*Hola, chicas,*" Eliza said, in her best imitation of Jacqui.

Mara looked up at the sound of Eliza's voice. Eliza was wearing her Sally Hershberger jeans and the discount Missoni top. Jacqui had covered her fauxhawk with the Pucci scarf. Mara was glad her friends each had a souvenir from the Mitzi closet.

"Let's talk, Mar," Eliza said bravely, when she got a little closer.

Mara nodded. "Yeah, that'd be good."

"You, too, Jac," Eliza said. "All of us. It's been too long."

The three of them ambled to the beach in silence, Jacqui walking between Mara and Eliza, hoping she could be the peanut butter to stick the three of them back together. They watched the seagulls glide gently over the waves and the ocean glitter under the setting sun. The hurricane had stirred up the ocean floor, and the beach was littered with broken seashells and assorted debris.

Finally, Eliza turned to Mara. "I'm really sorry. For everything. I really hope . . . I mean, I hope you know I would never do anything to hurt you," she said, her voice cracking. "I know you and Ryan are meant to be, and I made a mistake, and I'm really sorry. I wish I'd told you about Palm Beach earlier—I tried, but not hard enough. . . ."

" 'Liza, don't. Please don't cry," Mara said. "I was so awful to you at the fashion show, and I accused you of taking those stupid earrings. I'm so embarrassed. It's my fault too."

"No, really, it's me," Eliza said, wiping at her face with her whole palm. She reached down and blew her nose on the bottom of her gorgeous Missoni shirt. It was such an un-Eliza move that Mara and Jacqui had to laugh.

Mara nodded. "I trust you," she said simply. And, looking in her heart, she found that it was true. She really did trust Eliza. People made mistakes. She understood that now. And as happy as she was to be with Ryan again, her friendship with Eliza was just as important. You only met a few kindred spirits in your life, and you had to hold on to the ones you were lucky enough to find.

Eliza's eyes filled with tears again. In a hoarse voice, she said, "I hope you guys know you're the best friends I've ever had."

Jacqui slung an arm around each of their shoulders, and the three of them hugged each other tightly. Mara started to sob too, and without entirely totally knowing why, Jacqui did as well. They'd been so lonely without each other.

"Hey, look . . ." Jacqui said, pointing to some trash that had washed up on the beach. "Doesn't that look like our bottle?"

Mara almost couldn't believe it, but it was the same rum

bottle they'd hidden their message in at the start of the summer. What were the chances?

Eliza pulled the cork open and fished out the label. On top of the scrap was their note: *Hello from Mara Waters, Eliza Thompson, and Jacarei Velasco in the Hamptons. We're having the summer of our lives. If you find our bottle, please write your name and a note and toss it back into the ocean.*

Scrawled on the bottom of the page was the following:

Hello from Nova Scotia, Canada, from Sandra Shepherd, Alana King, and Margritte Lyon. We found your bottle floating in White Point Beach. We're having an amazing summer, too!

Jacqui, Eliza, and Mara laughed. It was like a little miracle.

"Nova Scotia! God, that's far away," Eliza said.

"The hurricane probably pushed it farther," Jacqui surmised. "Or brought it back."

"I wonder if they're like us," Mara mused, touching her neck. The Mikimoto pearl necklace. Mitzi had said it was hers to keep at the start of the summer. It was the only real gift from the designers. Mara thought of a certain tall redheaded sister of hers who would love it.

"Next summer—we'll be back!" Eliza declared. "Next summer— I know this sounds so cheesy, but I promise—it'll be the best summer yet. It'll be the summer of our lives."

Jacqui and Mara smiled indulgently. They were all thinking of the Internet ad that had gotten the three of them together in the first place. Would they au pair for the Perrys again? It was hard to say. Ryan had told Mara about little cottages you could rent down on the beach. Eliza was already planning her next internship, maybe for a fashion designer—she'd had enough of nightclub hostessing. And Jacqui . . . well, Jacqui was just thinking of how cute Kit had looked yesterday, and of making her dreams of NYU come true.

The day after the hurricane, the world was still, and at peace. It was a cleansing, a catharsis. The Hamptons would survive: During the fall the roads would be repaired, the monstrous houses rebuilt, and, come May, a new crew of hopefuls looking for fun and sun would come to play, fall in love, and drink too much champagne on the sandy white beaches.

Mara, Jacqui, and Eliza vowed that they would be back. Next summer would be here before they knew it.

acknowledgments

Thanks to Les Morgenstein, Josh Bank, Ben Schrank, and everyone else at Alloy for their wit, wisdom, and encouragement.
Thanks to Emily Thomas, Jennifer Zatorski, Tracy van Straaten,
and Rick Richter at Simon & Schuster for the wonderful sup-
port. Thanks to Deborah Schneider and Cathy Gleason for the
thoughtful guidance.

Much love and thanks to all my family and friends, especially
the DLCs; Bert, Ching, and Francis de la Cruz; Aina, Steve, and
Nicholas Green; the Johnstons; Dennis, Marsha, John, Anji,
Alexander, Tim, Rob, Jenn, and Valerie, and all the rest of the
Ongs, de la Cruzes, Torreses, Gaisanos, and Izumis out there.
Thanks to Kim De Marco, Deborah "Diva" Gittel, Thad and
Gabby Sheely, Tristan Ashby, Gabriel Sandoval, Liz Craft, Caroline
Suh, Tyler Rollins, Karen Robinovitz, Andrey Slivka, Katie Davis,
Tina Hay, Tom Dolby, Lisa Marsh, Alyssa Giacobbe, Sarah Eisen,
Jason Oliver Nixon, Andrew Stone, Paige Herman, Juliet Gray,
Shoshanna Lonstein Gruss, and Ed "Jean-Luc" Kleefield.

Thanks to the Flatotel, Khrystine Muldowney at Chanel, Siren PR, Norah Lawlor, and everyone at Lawlor Media Group for the fabulous New York launch. Thanks to Citrine, Nadia, Meredith, and everyone at Wagstaff Worldwide for the awesome West Coast party.

Thanks to everyone who dished and whose names I cannot mention here. You know who you are.

Last, I'd like to thank all of you who e-mailed, reviewed, and blogged about *The Au Pairs*. Thank you for your enthusiasm and good wishes. May all your summers be fun and scandalous!

about the author

MELISSA DE LA CRUZ is the author of many books, including *The Au Pairs* and her autobiographical teen novel *Fresh off the Boat*. She is also the coauthor of the tongue-in-cheek handbook to fashion *The Fashionista Files: Adventures in Four-Inch Heels and Faux-Pas*. Look for her next novel, *The Fortune Hunters*, and the forthcoming *Blue Blood* series in 2006.

Melissa has appeared as an expert on style, trends, and fame for CNN and the E! Entertainment Network and has written for *Glamour, Marie Claire, Harper's Bazaar, Teen Vogue, Cosmopolitan*, and *The New York Times*. She started her journalism career as a nightclub reviewer (and was once thrown out of a New York nightclub for giving it a bad review!).

She lives in Los Angeles with her husband, but considers herself bicoastal, since mentally, she's still in New York (and the Hamptons). You can e-mail her at hamptonsaupairs@yahoo.com. And check out the Web site: www.theaupairs.com.

not enough fun, sun, and romance? read on for a sneak peek at what the girls are doing next summer in the au pairs: *sun-kissed*.

"Can I help you?" Jacqui asked the new girl.

The girl looked at the three of them, as if noticing them for the first time. "Oh my God!" she said. "You're *them*!"

"Them who?" Mara asked, turning to her friends with a confused expression.

"You're *famous*!" The girl shrieked. "You guys are the coolest girls in the Hamptons—I read all about you in *Teen Vogue*!"

Last summer, as a favor to Mitzi Goober, the three of them had been featured in a "Summer Hotties" roundup in the magazine. Mara had been pictured on Garrett Reynolds's arm, stepping out of a Bentley, while Eliza had been photographed in her sequined Sass and Bide minidress holding a clipboard in front of a nightclub. There was even a double-page centerfold of Jacqui in the outfit she'd worn for the finale of the fashion show.

"You're Mara, right?" the girl said, thrusting a hand toward Mara. "The one with the hottest boyfriend in town."

"And you must be Eliza—the trendy one," she said, turning to Eliza.

"So that makes you Jacqui—my favorite!" She squealed, throwing her arms around a stunned Jacqui.

Mara and Eliza nudged each other, while Jacqui looked amused. "Favorite"? What were they, like, characters in a television show?

The new girl looked like she was about to faint. "How cool is it that I'm going to be working with you this summer!"

"Working with us?" Eliza asked, her eyes narrowing, grinding the cigarette butt with the bottom of her shoe.

"Well, with Jacqui, at least. I'm Shannon Shin. The new au pair! And I'm ready for the best summer of my life!"